Mayan
Countdown
2012

William Clyde Beadles

Cover art by Robin C. Beadles, *robinbeadles.com*

Author photo by Scott Beadles

Printed in the United States of America

ISBN 978-0-615-61692-6

To Tom and Scott, now and forever,
the delight and pride of my life.

Mayan Countdown

By William Clyde Beadles

I stood inside the dark, musty chamber of a 4,000-year-old Mayan temple in the jungles of Honduras, staring into a polished stone monolith about eight or nine feet tall that was reflecting what appeared to be my full lifelike image. The stone's surface was so highly polished that the image appeared three-dimensional. I was startled and curious at the same time. It looked as if my reflection could walk right out of the stone and confront me.

The surface of the stone was so clear and transparent that its surface seemed to not exist. I felt I could walk through it and encounter the image on the inside. Behind the reflected image of myself, I could see a myriad of pulsating star-like specks almost like the entire Milky Way was contained within the rock.

I suddenly realized it wasn't really my physical image that was being reflected. The image I saw was different; it almost didn't seem human, but it still looked like me... yet it had an eerie luminosity, a soft glow or brightness to it that was somewhat surreal. My reflected image was translucent, more like a ghostly image than a solid physical identical likeness. I had the impression that I was looking at my soul. Not my body; my soul. Sweat broke out and ran down the back of my neck. Adrenaline pumped through my veins like jet fuel. Frightened, terrified and confused all at the same time, I suddenly realized it must be my soul! But if this was my soul what did it want with me. Was my soul here to retrieve me beckoning me to follow its image into the rock and leave this life for some other? Standing there, I knew I had arrived at a pivotal point in my life.

Although a confrontation with death didn't feel eminent, I knew I was staring it in the face. The more I studied the image, the more uncomfortable and terrified I became. I felt physically paralyzed. For what seemed an eternity, yet was probably only seconds, nothing moved. I finally pulled together enough courage to reach out and touch the rock just to prove to myself that it was just a reflection. Mentally I prepared to make the first move and assure myself that my mind was just playing games with me. I reached out to touch the image, and it responded. It moved as I moved but in a mirror-like reverse motion. I started to regain my composure and confidence as the reflection moved exactly like a reflection should. As our fingers slowly moved toward each other's, approaching the mirror-like surface, I expected they would come to a stop when we ' touched.' To my surprise, they didn't. Our fingers *actually* touched. Stunned, I looked up into the face of the image and I saw my reflection smile back at me, but I was not smiling. I was too frightened at that moment to smile. I looked into its eyes. I felt its hand grasp me around the wrist. Mine coupled with his. I quickly looked down. I was holding onto myself in another world, another time, another place. My arm half in the rock and half out, I looked back to the eyes. I had forgotten to breathe. I sucked in a deep breath, continued to stare deep into the eyes of my reflective soul. I sensed I was being offered an option, a choice: I could continue on into the rock to join my soul to perhaps another life or stay and see what was still in store for me on this earth. My mind raced. I knew if I chose to stay, it would not be without its consequences. I wasn't ready to move into the next dimension of life's progression—whatever it might be. I had just made a major decision to change my life by coming to Choluteca, to stay in one place, to find meaning to my life. I relocated to Honduras just for that purpose. I was tired of running all over the world. I wasn't ready to travel to a new strange place. My decision to stop running was made. I didn't want to chase another story. Yet, maybe this was part of that great story I had always been searching for, maybe I was supposed to go. Or perhaps, I wasn't supposed to find the story... it was supposed to find me.

I decided not to run again but to stay. I looked once more into its eyes, I knew it understood. Within that moment, we communicated but not a word was spoken. I pulled my hand back, I knew there was more to learn and much more to understand within a very short time.

How I actually ended up in the jungles of Honduras at first was a bit of a mystery to me. After many years as a CBS news correspondent covering major international news stories, wars, insurrections, civil unrest, genocide, starvation, assassinations, government cover-ups, global screw-ups of every dimension, I became fed up with the state of journalism and with the current state of mankind. I wanted to escape it all, to find a life that had more meaning and depth.

Up until now my life had been made up of a series of snippets on local and national news broadcasts. I'd been to more than 130 countries, some of which don't even exist anymore. At age thirty-five, I had experienced more than most people would ever dream of experiencing. Millions of viewers around the world recognized my name, Thomas Clayton, and face from my daily CBS News reports. Although I was financially secure, my personal life and sense of being were well below the poverty line.

Traveling the world in a suitcase year in and year out, jumping every day from one place to another, had taken its toll on me. I just couldn't do it anymore. Maybe I was chasing all the wrong stories. I decided to make a major change. I still wanted a challenge, but I also wanted a life.

Maybe my 'big story' was looking for me but couldn't catch up with me. Maybe I didn't need to chase the world looking for that big story; maybe I really did need to stand still for a while and let that big story find me. What I needed to do was to find a place and settle down. I needed to find me.

During all my travels, one place kept pulling at me; it was as if my inner- compass, my DNA North Star, my internal magnetic, north kept pointing to Honduras, specifically a small jungle and ranching community inland from the Pacific Ocean called Choluteca.

I covered a follow-up story for CBS News about the reconstruction efforts after the massive devastation caused by a hurricane a few years ago. The intensity of the hurricane destroyed many parts of Honduras, including much of the tiny town of Choluteca. During that powerful storm, more than 11,000 people were killed in Honduras, Nicaragua, Guatemala and El Salvador. I was one of the first journalists into the area immediately after the storm. It had been a painful and heart-breaking story to cover.

A year later on the anniversary of that hurricane, I returned to Honduras for the second time to do the follow up story for CBS. During that assignment, I took a side trip to Choluteca. I was only there for two days, but I left with some kind of strange attachment to the people and the tranquility that I experienced while I was there. It reminded me a lot of Hawaii, except everything was in Spanish.

On the day I left Choluteca, I knew I would be back. I didn't know why, but it was as if I had missed something or was about to leave something behind. Later, I learned that this was a premonition of what lay ahead for me. I had much to learn and even more to understand about how and why I was drawn to Choluteca. All I knew was that my human antenna was picking up a signal, loud and clear from Choluteca.

My mind poured through my life trying to make sense of what I was experiencing. I popped back into the present and found myself backing away from the rock while my reflection watched. I knew that I had received a glimpse into the future.

Almost like a vision that had no visuals—a voice that had no sound—an understanding came to me. I was left with one thought. I sensed that the original concept of a true millennium was still alive. This was a gift I was given.

The Y2K millennium we all knew, with all of its predictions, had come and gone. For some it was a great relief, for others it was a disappointment. Within weeks it was old news and life went on. The end of the world was yet another media hyped event that turned out to be all hype and no substance. I felt time on this earth was still rapidly counting down to a dramatic climax, yet no one knew it. The secret was right here in this ancient Mayan Temple. The millennium hadn't missed us; it was still staring us straight in the face. The world was just using the wrong calendar.

This is why I was drawn to this particular spot on the globe.

But, what was waiting for me in my search to find my inner-self? What was the answer to the 'Big Story' that had eluded me? The story that I had been chasing? It was the beginning of December 2012. I felt the story was closing in on me.

The countdown had begun.

CHAPTER 1

On the surface it was like any other morning. Yet something was wrong … but I wouldn't know what it was for two weeks. For now, it was just now.

Suddenly, conscious of the sun through the slats in the window of my bedroom, rays of warmth lined my body with prison stripes of light and shadows. Half of my body thought it was still night; the other half knew it was just the beginning of a new day. I stretched in three directions at once and tried to soak in the warmth.

The Honduran sun was descendant of an ancient Mayan God, *K'in*. The early Mayans believed him to be life and the power behind the creation; He was related to *Chak*, the God of rain and lightning, whose gentle fondness for the female earth Goddess was almost incestuous. Life to them was the beginning and the end. And everything in between. Only *K'in* who gave life had power. *K'in*, the sun, entered every man, woman and child radiating energy, love and eternal life. I could feel that warmth and energy entering me now as I rolled over to see the light breaking through the trees, falling through the windows onto my bed. Morning was a rebirth. And for a few groggy moments, I, too, believed that I was privy to the keys of life, the answer to happiness and the manna that feeds dreams to the early-morning risers.

"*Tomás . . . Tomás!*" broke the dream. The call came from the kitchen, with the aroma of hot coffee and Tida cakes.

"Okay. I'm up. I'm up. I'm coming," I roared out, internally cursing the shrill of Tida's voice. She came with the house. Or, should I say, the house came with Tida. Four hundred and fifty dollars a month and Tida. *Domingos* were her only days off. Sundays were my favorite days to sleep in.

Pushing back the covers, I unwillingly rolled out of bed. The coolness of the terra cotta tile rushed to my eyes and caused my body to tighten. Every muscle fell into place with each step. If it weren't for the sun and the shower, my body would never recover. Outside, the orange blossoms gave the air a syrupy quality. The humid, tropical, earthy smell and the sweet gentleness of the fragrant orange blossoms were true dichotomies of expectations. Much like today, it was beautiful and calm on the surface, yet incredibly deceptive.

The drive into town was another chance to daydream. I loved the drive. Some people thought I was crazy to live this far out, but I thought they were crazy to live too close.

Choluteca had chosen me and I was soon to know why. The first year went by fast. I anticipated my second would, too. Funny how you tend to organize everything: time, people, your day, your life. This ranching community was carved out of the dense Honduran jungle. Lush pastures with rich grasses grew back almost as fast as the cattle could eat them.

Large *haciendas* were the country homes for many wealthy ranchers, who also kept homes in the small town where their children would attend school.

For me, I liked living outside the city. The countryside, or, should I say, the jungle, was my escape from work and all the concerns that went with it. I liked the peaceful quiet of *Los Ranchitos*. It was only twenty-two kilometers from *Parque Central* in Choluteca, but it seemed light years away.

My Suburban dropped into passing gear as I scooted around a truck, loaded down with cedar logs, headed for Puerto Cortez. From there they would be loaded aboard a cargo ship and end up as coffee tables in someone's front room.

I was a little late, but I wasn't really concerned. Scott had set up a garden party to show off a new series of pastels that his wife Robin had just finished. Scott Hoggan was my closest friend in Choluteca. We met shortly after I arrived here.

This weekend Scott wanted to invite some of the more prominent members of the community and friends to be the first to see a new series of her work. I have to admit that I, too, sensed something special about her art but couldn't really identify what it was then. I think I was probably the last to figure it out. Scott was probably second to last, because when he told me, I really couldn't believe it at first. But when I put it all together, I felt a little embarrassed. Having been a journalist all my life, I think I should have had an idea about what I was seeing before anyone else. But I didn't.

Scott's house was just north of *Parque Central* in Barrio

Los Mochis which was where most of the prominent families of Choluteca lived. As I approached *Parque Central*, I turned to Calle Vasquez. The cobblestone street sent vibrations rumbling through my tires, up through the chassis to the steering wheel. I had to slow down to go around a young boy, pulling a handcart loaded down with *leña* (firewood), which he would sell door-to-door to the housekeepers. I tooted my horn as I passed, and he tipped his straw cowboy hat as a gesture of acknowledgment. I then noticed it was Carlos. I stopped and rolled down my window, "*Carlos, Carlos ven. Como estás?*"

"*Muy bien, Don Tomás,*" Carlos answered with his familiar smile. "*Y a donde anda este Domingo, Don Tomás?*"

He inquired to where I was going this Sunday morning, and I replied, "*A la fiesta* at the house of *Señor Hoggan.*" Carlos did occasional cleaning for me at the radio station I owned. He had a small house near where my transmitter site was located. He lived there with his mother, who took in washing, and his younger sisters, who went to school. When Carlos' father left to go north to the logging area near Danli, Carlos dropped out of school and assumed the role as the head of the household. His mom worked three days a week with the Hoggans, so he was very familiar with all of them.

"*Mi madre está trabajando* there today, *Don Tomás,*" Carlos explained.

Carlos and I would talk back and forth in a mix of English and Spanish. I was fluent in both as were others in Choluteca. It was very common to hear the English/Spanish mix around town. At my radio station, my deejays played a mix of music and talk in a format that included Spanish and English. It was predominately Spanish, but I did offer 15-minute English newscasts on the hour at 7 a.m., noon and 7 p.m.

I told Carlos to come by the station on Monday because I had some work for him, adding that I would be sure to tell his mom I saw him when I got to the Hoggans. I waved goodbye, headed up the cobblestone street, turned and reached the square at *Parque Central*.

Church was not over yet, so the *Parque* was not crowded. The vendors were just starting to set up. I observed the ice cream carts, taco wagons and a half dozen *señora*s in colorful blouses and skirts with large tin bowls filled with tostadas and taquitos. I noticed the cloth towels laid across the tops to keep out the heat and the flies. This was cattle country, and I swear some of the flies were the size of small birds. I loved the tostadas. Some Sundays I would sit in the park at the *barra* and drink cold Imperial Beer and buy the tostadas from the colorful ladies.

Under a giant rosewood tree, the melon man carved his melons into baskets shaped like animals. Choluteca was the melon capital of Honduras. The climate and soil were perfect and the melon man knew just when to pick them to achieve the greatest flavor and sweetness. He had baskets shaped as jaguars, rabbits, iguanas, birds and, my favorite, the armadillo. He filled them with different mixtures of red, yellow, green and orange melon balls and cubes. Some he mixed in other fruits, dates, coconuts and flowers. He was an artist, the famous melon man. During the week, he would take special orders for family get-togethers, birthdays, *quince-ñeras*, weddings and any other special occasion. He also had mangos on a stick that all the kids loved. The adults liked the sliced mangos with chili pepper, salt and lime.

The cathedral on the eastside of *Parque Central* was *La Iglesia San Antonio*. To me it was one of the most beautiful Catholic churches in Central America. The priests had painted it a pale yellow with white borders around the windows and doorways.

In the evenings when the doves and the wild parrots returned to nest in the giant oak trees, *K'in*, the Honduran Sun, would fall upon the face of *La Iglesia San Antonio*. It was one of the most beautiful, peaceful sights you could imagine. The yellow and white complimented the soft setting rays of *K'in* and, for a few moments at each day's end, the building seemed to be a reflection of the magnificent Mayan God, *K'in*.

I pulled to a stop and looked up and down the Pan American Highway. All clear. I made a left onto the highway and passed over the bridge that spanned the Choluteca River. Down below I could see women and children. The kids were swimming and playing in the river as their moms, sisters and aunties washed clothing in the muddy brown waters.

From this vantage point, I could look down upon the dense jungle treetops and see giant iguanas sunning themselves. Even they appreciated the power of *K'in*. Like all cold-blooded lizards, iguanas soak in the sun to raise their body temperatures. Iguanas make good pets and in the local markets they were sold for food. Somewhere, somebody was just sitting down to a nice iguana lunch. I preferred the pet route. Back at *Los Ranchitos*, I had my own iguana. Like Tida, the iguana came with the house. Tida named him after her fat uncle, who in Spanish was also named *Tio Gordo* because all he did was eat, drink and sleep. Every morning *Tio Gordo* would run along the open beam rafters of the main room in my house and wiggle through an opening in the tiles on the roof. He then would crawl outside, up to the top of the roof, to sun. Every night he returned the same way.

As I got to the other side of the bridge and headed north to Scott's, I was reminded of a little bit of history I learned from *Padre Jesus*, who, I am sure, would be at the party later in the afternoon after he had finished his church duties.

The original site of Choluteca was built on the north side of the river, but it was the constant target of the Pacific pirates who would sail into the Gulf of Fonseca and up the Choluteca River to raise hell and stock up on supplies.

During one drunken night, the pirates drained the city of rum, wine and *aguardiente*, the locally made "white lightning." The town folks got into a fight with the drunken pirates, and the pirates returned the favor by burning the town to the ground. In the morning the pirates were gone, the city was gone, and the locals moved over to the south side of the river where the present town of Choluteca is today.

"Damn!" I yelled to myself as I swerved almost entirely off the road, barely missing a head-on collision with a bunch of young marines in a Humvee. Those sons-a-bitches think they are above the law and maybe they are. Honduras has a long history of involvement with the United States. Costa Rica, on the other hand, was always strong enough to resist U.S. interference in their affairs. Panama, however, until we turned over the Canal Zone, was ankle deep in U.S. red tape, but the United States ruled Nicaragua until the government threw them out.

Honduras never had a chance. The United Fruit Company moved into the northeast coast building railroads and banana plantations. Soon after, mining companies, construction companies and the U.S. military moved in to "help" this "poor defenseless country." Corruption and greed were rampant between the Americans and the Honduran leaders. After the U.S. pulled out of the *Contra*-backed involvement during the Reagan administration, the drug enforcement groups moved in. They had a headquarters on the island of Amapala for years, but to the chagrin of the residents of Choluteca, the U.S. government decided to build a high-tech traffic-control area on the southern outskirts of Choluteca. At first the local leaders thought it would be a boost to the local economy, but it has been nothing but a headache since they moved in.

I carefully pulled back onto the road and saw the marines disappearing from sight in my rear-view mirror.

Camp Semilla was the name given to the compound that the U.S. military was building under a joint agreement between the D.E.A. and the Honduran national Police Federation's Drug Enforcement Detail. *Semilla* means seed or, more literally, the fruit of cannabis (marijuana).

The United States government's first move was to fence

the area, about four square miles with over 100,000 feet of double-fenced, high-security chain link. One hundred feet inside the compound were surveillance cameras on towers spaced every 200 feet. A two-lane blacktop road, which was routinely patrolled by young leatherneck conquistadors in their armed Humvee, paralleled the perimeter fencing. Up 'til last week, only helicopters were seen flying in and out of the base. They must have completed the airstrip though, because last Wednesday four cargo jets flew in and, on Thursday: six more. The whole town was buzzing with curiosity. I was sure this would be the main topic of conversation at Scott's party.

I pulled off the Pan American and followed a dirt road about a mile to the entrance of Scott's ranch. It was a beautiful, modern Spanish-style hacienda with a small adobe barn. Horse pastures lead up to the house on both sides of the road. The house sat on top of a small hill or *lomas*. Dense stands of cedar, rosewood, oak, tamarind and palm groves surrounded the property, a perfect hiding place for the giant cats of the jungle, *El Tigre* or *Pantera*, more commonly known as jaguars and panthers. The jaguar, the largest cat in the Americas, measures up to two meters in length. Scott worried about his horses and was always on guard for the big cats. About three years ago, Scott told me a large cat dragged off one of his horses. Jaguars are powerful, impressive hunters. They have no fear—just cunning, stealth-like skills. They also drive ranchers crazy by hauling off cattle. They have been known to kill manatees in the slow-moving swamp areas of the *selva* and even take on a crocodile or two.

They are perfectly camouflaged with brown fur and black spots. The all-black jaguar (*La Pantera*) is most often seen in the provinces of Olancha and *Gracias a Dios* in the dense jungle that borders Nicaragua but hasn't been seen in this area for years.

The other predators are the cougars *El Puma* or mountain lions. They are about half the size of the large jungle cats but more of a menace. Around the ranches, they eat sheep, chickens and domestic pigs. They are brown with no spots, but have large black paws that provide sturdy footing for mountainous and rocky areas in *las lomas*. Since cougars are great jumpers, a fence is a joke for protection. They easily can jump a fence or straight up into a tree with a single leap. Some have been known to jump as far as 20 meters. Maybe that is one of the reasons the Mayans believed that they were possessed with mystical powers. Twenty meters is more than 60 feet the length of two first downs in football terms.

Whatever the lions and cougars leave behind, the *sopelotes* clean up. Of all the birds in Central America, these large, meat-eating vultures are the ugliest. The *sopelotes* are nature's Hoover vacuums, cleaning right down to the bone the left-over carnage of the jungle cats. They also have an uncanny sense to single out the weak and the sick. They hover in the air, circling their target until it is dead. Whenever a vulture circles overhead, there is a meal below.

I parked my truck and walked around to the passenger side to see if I had done any damage when I had to drive half on and half off the road. All this because those crazy marines were out for their joy ride! Luckily, it was mostly mud splashed all down the side. Nothing to worry about, but I'd love to get my hands around the neck of that punk driver.

Scott's door was open, so I strolled in and was immediately almost run down by Scott's youngest son chasing another boy through the house, out the door and onto to the front lawn. Two near misses in one day. I better be careful. They say things come in threes.

"Hi, Thomas. Come on in," I heard as I turned back around to see Robin.

"What did you feed those boys—pure sugar?" I chuckled and looked back to see Stephen tackle his buddy and roll over and over on the front lawn.

"No, they've been wild all morning. Guess it's all the commotion," Robin replied.

I continued through the house, out to the back patio area, where everyone was gathered.

I needed a drink to calm me down. Those crazy marines still had me pissed off and I could use a good, cool relaxing drink. I was also anxious to hear the latest gossip about the military's shenanigans and why everyone was getting edgy. Something wasn't right. Something wasn't above board. I sensed it and so did everyone else.

william clyde beadles

CHAPTER 2

Scott was a wonderful man. At first appearance, he seemed quite gentle and soft-spoken. He was an accomplished archeologist and a leader in his field. He was surprisingly different as you got to know him. His sense of humor was catching and his approach to life was always positive and confident. For a man that spent so much time studying the past, he had a real sense about where he was going. When we talked about ancient times, I would sometimes get a little confused because it almost sounded like we were talking about the future. He told me once, "Time is the only science that, if you study it long enough, it will kill you."

He had four children, two girls and two boys. The oldest, Laura, was in high school, one year ahead of her brother Brian. Stephen was in seventh grade, and Lori, the baby a special girl—was just starting fourth grade. Lori was the sweetest little girl I think I had ever known. Lori had just been diagnosed with an advanced case of incurable leukemia. Scott and Robin loved and suffered a lot over this child and had not told the other children what was about to happen to their sister. Sometimes life just doesn't make sense. How can a disease so ugly take control of something so beautiful and innocent?

Scott had a beautiful home. Robin's special artistic touch could be seen throughout. His wife was a true, natural-born artist with an exceptional empathy for people. Robin's talent for capturing the lifestyles and emotions of the local people, plus the places that she enjoyed, showed in her art. The people of Choluteca took a special and unusual immediate love for her and her work. She had a small gallery off the main square of *Parque Central* and catty-corner to *La Iglesia San Antonio*. Every time she put out a new painting, for some unexplained reason, almost the entire town would pass by and quietly admire what she had created.

The backyard was filled with guests. Most of them I knew but not all. Scott had a large patio area with a stone river-rock fire pit and barbecue. He had catered the food from *El Rincon* Restaurant. It was the local favorite, central gathering place and waterhole in town. Amaya, the owner, was the woman in my life. She had to stay back at the restaurant that night to cater another large group that had rented out her restaurant for a wedding reception. I missed having Amaya with me—especially on occasions like this. We spent as much time together as possible, but it was never enough for me. I was still a little bit intimidated by Amaya's beauty and strong, magnetic personality. Not that I should be. I have traveled the world and have had my share of relationships in almost every country, but somehow she was the most intriguing, exotic woman I had ever met. My own feelings for her scared me. When I arrived in Honduras over a year ago, I didn't expect to meet a woman so soon, let alone one like Amaya. Actually, I didn't think a woman like Amaya even existed anywhere but in a man's wildest dreams. She was a tigress in a gazelle's body with the cunning of a female wolf. She was both a challenge and a gift. I had to decide if I was the man for her. She had already chosen me.

Eduardo, the head chef, and his brothers had a couple sides of beef rotating over the pit and skewers of lamb, chicken and shrimp on the barbecue. Amaya had sent them to handle Scott's party. On the grill *Eduardo* also had whole pineapples, their skins sliced off. Rows of corn still in their green husks were being smoked in the charcoal oven, along with an assortment of local vegetables. On the sides of the barbecue were long built-in stone serving tables laden with salads, breads and, of course, beautiful carved melon baskets of fruit from the melon man. The smoky aroma from the barbecue filled the air, as did the natural fresh smells of blossoms from the jacaranda and almond trees. Tables with white umbrellas were scattered around the patio. From the pool came splashing and giggles of the smaller guests.

The *Rincon* group was planted around the outside bar at the other end of the pool. Scott had a local craftsman build this portable bar from split cane and natural calf leather with a rosewood-varnished top. It was ten feet long and only approachable from the front because at either end were a matched pair of Brahma bull horns that acted like bookends to hold the line of drinkers in place across the front of the bar. Hooked over one horn to the right side of the bar was Lazaro's sombrero. He was hatless, with *K'in* beating down on his balding head, his belly to the bar and his fist clinched tightly around his *Ron con Coca-Cola*. Lazaro was the local M.C. and had his own music groups who played at various parties like this gathering. At the other end of the bar, in deep debate, were the mayor, several ranchers and Colonel Royale. As I assumed, their topic of conversation was all about what was going on at Camp Semilla.

"The only mission that we have is to set up a joint authority for the Central American nations to control and eradicate the *narco traficanates*. Los gringos are deeply committed to the Central American Federation and, with the cooperation of our government, we will prevail," said Colonel Royale.

"At first I thought this would be good for the economy of the whole city, but it has had little impact on that matter. What concerns us are why are so many of their missions taking them into the mountains and areas to the north of Choluteca?" said the mayor.

"*Sí Señor,*" jumped in one of the ranchers. "Last week I found the fences down on two areas of my property where those *marinos* and their vehicles have passed over my land. My workers repaired the fences, but it took us three days to round up the loose cattle. I still haven't found eight. We did find what was left of one that a *tigre* carried off. There are no *drogas* on my property, *señor*. So why are they here? What I did find was some kind of monitoring device in three areas near the back of my ranch's northeast side. They were spread across a meadow at the mouth of Solidad Canyon. They look like metal posts with a single antenna coming out of the top. I want to know what they are doing out there is what."

Colonel Royale replied, "They are simply on training missions, but I will report this to the base commander on Monday."

"Yeah, I found one the other day on my ranch, too. What right do they have to just come on my land and do whatever they want?" said another rancher.

I asked the bartender for a *cerveza* and joined into the conversation "It sounds like these pipes are monitoring devices, but what are they monitoring? If they were only on training missions, they wouldn't leave these devices behind, Colonel. There must be more to this story than you are letting on. Do you or don't you know what these devices are?"

"*Tomás*, I do not know," said Royale.

"You don't know or you can't say?" I shot back abruptly.

"*Sí Señor, diganos*! Let's hear it!" responded several of the men as the debate started to escalate.

Unlike the sweaty brow of Lazaro, Colonel Royale was cool as a cucumber, but I did detect a slight stiffening of his body language.

"I do not know, but if it will make you feel better, I will inquire this afternoon and report my findings at *El Rincon* tomorrow morning when I see you," said Colonel Royale.

Just then, south of the ranch streaked four stealth fighters banking to the east and, two-by-two, landing gear down, disappeared under the treetops as they touched down at Camp Semilla. The whole party looked to the skies to watch the never before seen, bat-like aircraft swoop down and disappear into the jungle canopy.

"*Cabron, hermano!*" exclaimed the mayor. "What the hell are those?"

"They are part of the tactical air support that we were promised by the United States. They will be flying missions out of our base here in support of our ground troops, fighting the *narco traficantes*," boasted Colonel Royale.

As the crowd settled back into the fiesta, I looked at the stunned faces of the men I had just been talking with. I didn't trust the colonel, and I knew they didn't either. My journalistic background had heard this kind of government-double talk one too many times. How could Colonel Royale be the head liaison officer for the Honduran joint projects and not know what those surveillance devices were? He either knew or, for security purposes, would not say . . . or our government was up to some other covert operation.

Those bat-like aircraft were tactical fighters called F-1000s, the latest nuclear global attack fighters capable of Mach IV. They also had the ability to hover in a silence mode at any altitude above 300 feet. They could level a city or slice a finger off a soldier more than five miles away with an array of lethal laser technology. They were first tested in the Southwest United States during the '60s and were finally tied to numerous UFO sightings throughout the country. They were far too lethal and sophisticated to simply be here to support the fight against narcotic traffickers. It would be like using a 12-gage shotgun for a fly-swatter. Their bat-like appearance reminded me of the myths of the bats in Mayan cosmology. They were connected to the underworld or the death cycle.

I got another drink and left the debate, wandering over to look at Robin's art. She had about a dozen new pieces framed and set on easels along the covered veranda across the back of the house. Robin had a special ability to capture realistic colors in her art. Her subjects seemed very life-like. She traveled the city and the countryside, photographing people. Then returning to her small studio, she turned them into these magnificent pieces of living art. I was looking at one titled *The Amazing Maize Man*. We all knew him because he was always at the main market just east of *Parque Central*.

El Mercado Merced was filled with kiosks, and they sold everything: food, pots and pans, cloth, live chickens, iguanas, soap, perfumes, hats, leather goods, flowers, plants, seeds, canned goods, breads, cookies, candies, fish, meat, and pharmaceuticals. The market ran seven days a week, rain or shine. The amazing maize man had split 55-gallon drums in half, lengthwise, to create his own oven barbecues. They were filled with glowing orange, gray charcoal smoking bushels of corn in green husks. He rotated the cobs of corn by hand to lightly brown the husks on all sides. In her painting, it was obvious his hands had been burned many times over.

Her next painting was one of three women carrying baskets of fresh-cut flowers on their heads, walking through the market. Other women sat to each side of them, sitting on stools, selling their baskets of fresh vegetables. I turned to the next one and saw a cobbler at work in his small stall. He was putting a sole on a shoe. A small boy looked on, maybe his son or his apprentice. To his side lay an array of tools he used in his trade, and hanging above him were leather belts and purses. Over his shoulder I could see a saddle with a wooden horn.

The next one was called *Domingos*. It was the *Iglesia San Antonio* with a padre at the door greeting the Sunday worshippers. Families gathered around the entrance to the large open wooden doors.

As I looked to the next one to my surprise—it was Carlos, pulling his small wooden handcart along a country road. The cart was filled with firewood to be sold in the city. It was appropriately titled "*Leña* to Market."

Another painting of a mother and father in the cathedral with their little daughter, who was receiving her first communion, as friends and family members looked on during this special occasion, caught my attention. The peace and pride radiated from each and every face. The light from outside poured down through the stained glass window of Jesus holding a little lamb, and the colors magically traveled through the air and fell like a kaleidoscope upon the little girl's white lace dress. It was another gift from *K'in*. Just as I turned, I heard Scott's voice to my side.

"She just finished that one last night," Scott said to me.

"Hi, Scott. Robin really has outdone herself this time. How's *Ciudad Blanca* going?" I said.

"Actually, Thomas, I think I've found something that may be of major importance, but I'm not sure. I would like you to come out to the site at *Xhutlan* and see something. When can you get away?" said Scott.

"How about Tuesday?" I asked.

"Great, Thomas, but first I have to show you that I finally am a celebrity of Choluteca too," said Scott.

He led me past a few more paintings to the one on the end of the veranda. It was the clearing at *Xhutlan* with Scott and some of his workers at the entrance to a small temple. Over the doorway was a stone-carved sun symbol and on the sides of the entrance two sets of carvings. To the left was *Chak* the God of Rain and Lightning; the Maize God, *Hun Hunahpa*, and *Chab* the Earth God. To the right were: a skull, a serpent, an alligator and a bat. Thick green vines covered most of the outside, and the jungle had swallowed everything around the temple. I had seen many of these symbols at other sites at Copan, Tikal, Chich'en Itza and Plaenque. Scott, however, could tell you the meaning of them all.

"Congratulations, can I have your autograph?" I said with a deep laugh.

"Knock it off. Come on, I'll get you another refill, and then I want to show you something out in my workshop," Scott said.

Next to his barn, he had a large workshop. The inside storage area was where he kept hundreds of artifacts he had uncovered over the years, a working museum of the past. Each year during the summer months, a great number of university students showed up and helped him with his excavations. They came filled with great expectations and learned that this type of work was slow and methodical. Scott worked them hard, and they always left with a thirst for more. Scott had taught me a lot about the great Mayan civilization, and I, too, had that thirst for more.

Today the Mayan number in the millions. It is estimated between eight to ten million are concentrated in a single area that includes the southern Mexican states of Tabasco, Chiapas, the Yucatan Peninsula on down to Central America in Guatemala, Belize, El Salvador and the southern most reaches of Honduras. Unlike the scattered tribes of North American Indians, and the various civilizations that have populated Mexico, the Mayans represent the single largest block of American Indians that ever lived. Having endured repeated cycles of conquest that still plague them today, they have a unique cohesiveness that holds them together both physically and spiritually.

The Mayans had a great devotion to cosmology. They were skywatchers and shamans whose journeys took them to other places in time easily moving between the under-world, the earthly world and the worlds that were mysti-cally beyond this one. They were time travelers who were obsessed with the concept of motion and change creating calendars far more exact than any others in the world. The Maya invented the concept of "Zero" in mathematics before any other civilization. They had many books—of which only four are known to have survived. One of these is the *Popol Vuh* which describes the creation myth. The *Popol Vuh* uncovers the Mayan secrets of cosmology, astronomical events and recounts the adventures and stories of the most important Mayan deities and heroes.

Unfortunately most of the written records of the Maya were destroyed by the conquistadores and the Roman

Catholic priests when they first invaded the Mayan empire. In the name of religion thousands of books and records were destroyed. Books that were written on a papyrus like bark and paper were burned in piles. Written history inscribed on metal plates flattened to leaf thin pages were melted down and lost forever.

No one really knows why such an advanced civilization all of a sudden just walked away from their cities in the jungles. They abandoned their great architecture, their art, farms, plantations, temples, celestial observatories and places of learning.

The Maya didn't disappear; they simply faded away into the surrounding mountains and rain forests leaving behind in ruins thousands of years of advanced learning.

One thing has always puzzled me. If the Maya were so advanced and educated, where did all of that knowledge and intelligence go? They were so ahead of their times in comparison to the rest of the world. Why didn't they just go some where else and start over? Whether they migrated or fled away, where did all of that advanced learning disappear to?

How can millions of Maya still exist today, but in such a humble and poverty ridden state of dismemberment? What happened to the great Mayan scholars, scientists, mathematicians, physicians, astronomers, medicine men and philosophers? How could have they lost all of that brain power? Where did they go? It was baffling.

As we walked into Scott's workshop, he said, "Sit down over here. Put your feet up, as if I had to offer."

I sat down into one of his overstuffed leather chairs, put my drink down on the table next to me, and stretched my feet out onto the large circular coffee table in front of me. "How's Lori doing? She looks like a playful porpoise in the pool."

"Doc said that she won't really start to get sick for a few more months. Then he says she will start to have problems keeping her food down. Robin and I still haven't been able to tell the others yet. We keep praying and hoping for some miracle, but it doesn't look good, Thomas," said Scott.

"Can't they do something for her stateside?" I said.

"Not really, Thomas. Doc says this particular leukemia is fatal. He has sent his pathology and oncology reports to everyone he could in the United States, but they all came back the same. He says when the time comes; we will just have to keep her as comfortable as we can. He says it is best to keep her here with us and her brothers and sister," said Scott. He looked away and swallowed, holding back the tears I knew were building inside of me, too.

"It's not fair. It just *isn't fair*. With all the scientific knowledge we have in this world today, it's still the little children that have to suffer," I said.

"Thomas, I know you're not a religious man. You told me once that religion is for people who don't want to go to Hell, but spirituality is for people who have been to Hell and don't want to go back. I know you are a spiritual person down under all that hunk-of-a-man," Scott said, as he looked into my eyes with his whimsical grin. "Just keep Lori in your prayers, and collectively we will all pray for a miracle."

Scott paused for a moment and said. "I've been working on the site at *Xhutlan* and every time I go to the temple of *K'in* at the end of the meadow I feel something weird pulling me. It's not a physical pulling; it's a spiritual pulling. It is as if there is something inside the temple that wants to reveal something to me. Perhaps it is a vortex? Much has been written in ancient and modern times about these magnetic, metaphysical attractions. It is like an energy field or a vibration that is so soft that you almost don't think it is there, but I *know* it is," Scott paused. I was pulled into his words. As I pondered what he had just said, Scott continued, "Thomas, I want you to come with me. I want to see what you see. What you experience. I'm missing something. Maybe you can help."

"You know I would be glad to Scott, but you know I'm afraid of the dark," I said jokingly.

Scott smiled and said, "Okay, Tuesday it is then. Bring your flashlight, you big wuss!" Scott stood up and asked me to follow him to the back of the shop where his office was. As we walked in, I sat down in front of his desk. He stepped over to his files and pulled out a folder.

"Inside the temple of *K'in* I found a wall mural. It is on the north façade of the inner wall of a room I just opened up. The entrance to the room had been sealed off from the grand room at the entrance of the temple. What is interesting," Scott said as he pulled from his file a floor plan he had made of the chamber "is that this room is the largest room in the temple. Steps lead down to the floor that is 30 feet below the entrance level and the ground outside. The room is perfectly square, 160 feet to a side. You enter from the south and as you descend the stairs, across the room on the north façade, you see the mural. What's odd about this room is what's in the center of it: there is a very large, irregular-shaped boulder. It is about 40 feet high and has a circumference of 120 feet. Steps have been carved into the boulder and lead to the top where there is, I assume, an observation platform that is square, six feet by six. All four walls tapered inward like a pyramid to a center point directly above the center of the six-foot-square observation platform. From there, you have a perfect view of the entire chamber, top to bottom. The mural is almost intact, but parts of it have been destroyed by water seepage. When we go on Tuesday, you'll see for yourself. If what I think I have found is true, it could be a very large, important archeological site. The mural talks about the future and the end of life, as we know it. It's kind of like a prediction of an Armageddon but it explains about promises or gifts that will come with the new cycle of life or the rebirth.

"The Mayans believe in life cycles; we are at the end of the fifth cycle. According to the Mayan calendar birth, growth, death and rebirth are each a cycle. It is also intrinsic in the philosophies of the great religions like the Buddhist and Hindus. The Julian and Gregorian beliefs are a linear approach to time with a definite beginning and end that is based on 1,000-year increments, a millennium concept. Remember all the hype concerning the end of the world as we approached the new millennium (Y2K)? What if their calendar is off by a few years? Thomas, the Maya Round

Calendar puts the end date of this life cycle on December 21, 2012. That is just two weeks away!"

"Wait a minute . . . wait a minute, if I hear you right, you're trying to tell me that, in two weeks, we could be facing Armageddon?" No sooner than I got the word "Armageddon" out of my mouth, the ground began to shake. I looked Scott straight in the eye and said "Earthquake!" It was a sharp jolt and then a rolling that lasted about fifteen seconds.

"Let's get out of here," Scott yelled and we exited through the back door to his office.

We half-ran and half-walked around to the front of the workshop out to the pool. Everyone was on his or her feet and chatting nervously.

"Is everyone okay?" Scott yelled out to his guest. Everyone nodded yes. "That was a lot stronger than the one yesterday, Thomas," Scott said. "It is either a new quake or yesterday's was just a precursor to today's … or a much bigger one yet to come."

Just then, I looked over near the barbecue area and saw two men helping the mayor up out of a pile of fruit and broken melon baskets. When the quake hit, the mayor was just getting a plate of fruit. He was so startled that he dropped his plate of fruit on the ground and slipped on the pieces, falling back toward the fruit table. He reached out to catch himself and grabbed the tablecloth, pulling down the fruit baskets on top of him. He was feeling no pain. The rum had taken care of that problem. He was even laughing as he was helped up. Scott ran to the mayor.

"Are you okay Enrique?" Scott blurted out. "I'm so sorry."

"*No, no, mi amigo,* I'm fine," said the mayor.

"Daisy, bring me some towels!" Scott shouted to Carlos's mom.

We lived on the edge of the Pacific Rim called the Ring of Fire, volcanoes and earthquakes were part of everyday life since time began here and a common occurrence in Central America. We had experienced a swarm of earthquakes over the last three months and some scattered volcanic activity.

As Daisy helped the mayor clean up, I told Scott, "This is one hell of a party, Scotty. First, we are invaded by bat-like fighters and then an earthquake." I jokingly warned Scott, "Don't forget, Scotty, things happen in threes. Just a warning . . . two down and number three to go!"

Scotty laughed out loud and said, "Look!" At the bar Lorenzo was still standing, but all alone. He didn't even feel the quake and he hadn't spilled a drop of his rum and coke.

I gave Scott an *abrazo* hug and thanked him for such a nice time, including all the added "entertainment."

"Let's pick up where we've left off on Tuesday. You've got my interest peaked now," I said, and turned to leave.

CHAPTER 3

M onday mornings, I always got a head start on my week, as did most of the leaders in Choluteca. It has been tradition here for many years to meet early each Monday at *El Rincon*. It was an informal town council and better business bureau rolled into one. Friday afternoons, the town leaders would regather to wrap up their weekly business – it was a great way to end the day – and the week. Some of the best stories were told on those Friday afternoons and sometimes they went well into Saturday morning.

El Rincon has always been the gathering place around *Parque Central*. More stories have been told over those worn-out wooden tables than there are stories in the Choluteca Library. If only those tables could talk!

"*El Rincon*" means the corner and, appropriately, the restaurant was on the corner of *Calle Morazon* and *Avenida Central*, directly across the park from the *Iglesia San Antonio*.

The entrance to the *El Rincon* sat on that corner flanked on both sides of the building by indoor-outdoor patios for patrons. They entered through two large, hand-carved mahogany doors with large rod-iron handles. Once inside your were greeted by *Don Pepe*. He was, I believe, the oldest living *maitre'd* in the world. Nobody, including himself, could remember his age. Yet despite his somewhat wobbly appearance, he was sharp as a tack and blessed with whit and charm rivaling those of Mark Twain. His neatly trimmed gray goatee rested gently beneath his stately Spanish nose, and his dark brown eyes, clear and bright, reflected a hint of a grin. He was the unofficial patriarch of the *Rincon* and guardian of Amaya after the death of her parents.

Amaya's parents bequeathed *El Rincon* to her, as her father's father had handed it down to them. Amaya's grandfather was Chinese, one of the first to come to Honduras. He and his wife had opened a small restaurant "*El Chino del Nuevo Mundo*." His wife died shortly after they first arrived. "*El Chino*," as locals knew him, married a young Indian girl from the north, Santa Rosa de Copan. Amaya's father was from that marriage. Her mother was the daughter of an Arab clothing merchant, who owned his own store.

With both her grandparents and parents gone, Amaya was the sole heir of her family's many years of hard work.

Amaya was blessed not only with a mix of nationalities but also with a strong business sense. Although in her early thirties, Amaya was very mature for her age. She had literally grown up at *El Rincon*. Attached to the restaurant was an outdoor, walled-in courtyard and behind that a two-story colonial style home she grew up in and still lived.

She never married—which pleased me, as Amaya and I

had somehow hit it off together the first time we met. It was just a little over a year ago. She was tall and slender, with silky long black hair, which fell to her waist and framed the most exotic face I had ever seen. She graduated from a private catholic school for girls, but never attended university. Right after high school she was thrown into the family restaurant business where she developed her own style of street smarts, business sense, wit and charm. The movers and shakers of Choluteca were drawn to *El Rincon*. She could hold her own with the best of them.

As I pulled up to park, I noticed the Mercedes, Land Rovers and dually pickups. I knew the owners of each and every one. I jumped down from my suburban and there, as always, was Orlando. With a bucket of soapy water and a sponge – and for only fifty cents he would turn my muddy truck into the sparkling chariot it should be. It would be waiting for me when I came out.

"*Buenos Días Tomás*," came the greeting from *Don Pepe* at the door.

"*Buenos Días, Don Pepe*," I replied.

"Looks like someone partied too much this weekend. Your *café* is waiting."

As I walked past *Don Pepe*, I could hear him whisper to himself out loud, " . . . and so is Amaya," followed by a slight chuckle. Even though her crew helped cater the party at Scott and Robin's, Amaya was not able to attend because she had to "hold down the fort" at *El Rincon*.

Everyone was mingling and talking from table to table. As I walked over to my usual place on the patio, Mario served me my first cup of coffee almost before I sat down. At the end table were three ranchers and the owner of the *Hotel Mirador*. At the table to my right sat "*El Alcalde*" the mayor of Choluteca, Enrique Lopez. He admired Scott and was always there to help him with whatever he needed. Sitting with the mayor was Colonel Esteban Royale, the head of the *Guardia Nacional*, and the owner of the only supermarket in town, Don Guillermo Gomez.

"*Tomás*, where is Scott?" asked the mayor.

"Probably still cleaning up the mess you made at his party," I joked. Everyone laughed, including the *Alcalde*.

At that moment in walked *Padre Jesus*, who sat down at my table as many in the room acknowledged his arrival with a "*Buenos Dias, Padre*."

Padre Jesus was a much-respected man of the cloth and probably knew more about the history of Choluteca than anyone alive. Most people considered him to be the resident historian of the town. Originally from Cuba, he came to Choluteca as a young priest in the early sixties. Although he didn't know it then, he was about to experience the most exciting chapter in the history of Choluteca—not to mention the world.

"Missed you at Scott's yesterday," I told him.

"I had a busy day, more so than normal. Our services are growing larger and larger. I'm seeing a lot more *campesinos* especially for the midday mass. Yesterday, we actually had people outside. I had to turn on the outside speakers!" said *Padre Jesus*.

"You must be pleased," I replied. "What do you think is

attracting them in such large numbers?"

"I have a feeling that . . ." before *Padre Jesus* could finish, he was interrupted by Colonel Royale, who stood to speak to the group.

"Yesterday I stopped off at the base and talked with Commander Perry. I told him about your concerns, and he has assured me that the metal posts are simple movement sensors, which can monitor any motion that occurs five to eight feet above ground. If a vehicle, an upright walking man, or even a man on horseback passes one of these sensors, it triggers an alert. He said they are placed five feet above the ground, so they will not pick up movement by animals, which would trigger false readings. The motion sensors will pick up any *narco traficantes* who pass one. The trucks and Humvees that you have seen are equipped with receivers to monitor the field posts placed throughout the countryside," the colonel said.

"What about my broken fences and missing cattle?" inquired one of the ranchers.

"The commander said he would pay for the damages, and he extends an apology for your inconvenience. He also assured me that if they need to go on to your property, they will advise you in advance. He wants you to know that these are training exercises and their success is beneficial for all of us," said the colonel.

I leaned back in my chair and thought to myself, 'I've heard this all before. It appears he really doesn't know but *something* is going on at that base and it doesn't involve drugs. For some reason, the U.S. military is not telling the colonel the entire story.' The rest of the group began to all talk among themselves about the *marinos* and what was going on.

Amaya walked up behind me, placing her hand on my shoulder, leaning down to whisper in my ear, "Hi, *mi Amor*."

I reached up and took her hand and guided her into the chair between *Padre Jesus* and me.

"Scott called and said he wouldn't be able to make it this morning," Amaya told us both.

"Yeah, he had a long day yesterday. It was quite a party," I said.

"So I've heard," replied Amaya.

"Sounds like you and I missed out," said *Padre Jesus*. "I really wanted to see Robin's new paintings, but I'll have to pass by her shop and see them with the rest of the town."

"There are a couple that you'll really like I'm sure," I told the padre, remembering "*Domingos*" and "First Communion."

"Excuse me *Padre*, can I steal Thomas away for a minute?" Amaya begged.

"*Por supuesto mi hija*," replied *Padre Jesus*.

"Excuse me," I said, as I got up to follow Amaya back to her office. I loved the way she walked, confidant but gracefully. Not to mention her fine little, sexy butt. She closed the door behind me and, with one move, had her arms around my neck and her lips on mine. My arms slipped comfortably around her waist. Her long silky hair tickled the hair on my arms. She leaned her head back and said, "I missed you yesterday."

"And I missed you too," I said giving her another kiss and

hug. Her head hung on my shoulder and in my ear she softly spoke, "You know we don't have to be alone so much, don't you?" I could feel her permissive nature and see that innocent look on her face without actually looking at it.

I whispered back, "You'd get bored with me if you had me all to your own." Teasingly, I added, "Besides, that kind of arrangement takes a lot of planning and you know how I hate all that planning."

She pulled back and put her hands on my cheeks, pulled my face close to hers and said, "Thomas, we could do it right now. You've got your own personal priest sitting out there at your own table eating his breakfast with nothing to do." She gave me a peck and moved back a step laughing. "Besides, we both know Tida does all your planning! Now get out of here before your breakfast gets cold!" She gave me a pat on my butt as I turned and walked back to the patio to finish breakfast.

I bid my farewell to the group and walked out of *El Rincon*. There waiting for me was my red chariot. Sparkling clean. Only fifty cents ago it was a muddy mess, but Orlando had done his magic. As I pulled out, I looked down the street and saw Robin at the end of the block going into her shop. She drops the kids at school and then goes into work. She picks the kids up after school, and they go back to their ranch. She has a small studio at her shop where she works on her art during the day until she closes up at 3 p.m. Saturdays she is open all day but has help to run the shop.

I headed to the radio station's studios located just east of town. I bought it a little over a year ago from an American guy that wanted to retire and move to Miami. I was look-ing for something to keep me busy after I left CBS. I had grown despondent over the state of journalism in the United States and really felt that it was a dying profession. When I first started in journalism, I wanted to be a field reporter for a major network. By the time I got the chance most of my idols in the business had long since retired. Advertising revenues and audience ratings had turned the news profes-sion into an actor's guild. Young, good-looking teleprompter readers had replaced seasoned, tough, hard-hitting journal-ists who took their profession with zeal. News became big business and television and radio stations became commod-ities. Networks and individual stations were being traded like monopoly pieces and the men and women who built the news were shoved aside by financial "geniuses," Wall Street gurus and investors with little or no knowledge of broad-casting. The radio business was filled with mom-and-pop operations that quickly sold out to the networks that were buying up the industry. The Wall Street Shamans descended with their smoke and mirrors and waltzed away with the FCC licenses in hand, leaving behind the original owners who sold their souls for pennies on the dollar.

The very government that promised freedom of speech had changed the ownership laws so that thousands of licenses ended up in the hands of the few. News became part of the programming department. The programming department became a subject of the king: SALES. One net-work owner told me that every person, from the janitor to the general manager, works for the sales department. The members of the sales team generally were the highest paid and there was a reason for that: bottom line and keeping the shareholders happy. I hung on for a few years, hoping I could get that "big story" that would wake everyone up, but that was just a dream. Journalism as I knew it was dead. I have to admit though that I still have the fever to write that last one big story. 'Wake up Thomas. You're heading off into never-never land again', I told myself. A pothole jarred me back into reality. I pulled up in front of the station and parked. Inside Carlos was waiting for me along with the receptionist.

"Good morning, everyone," I said.

"Good morning, *Tomás*," said Carlos.

"Antonio wants to see you as soon as he can," said Carla, picking up an incoming call. "*Buenos Días, Radio Onda, como puede dirijer su llamada . . . bueno . . .* the engineer wants to see you too," she said after putting the caller on hold.

"Okay Carla. Carlos come with me," I said. "I saw your mom. Did she tell you about *El Alcalde*?"

"Yes *Tomás*, seems like *El Alcalde* enjoyed *la fiesta* a little too much," Carlos replied.

Turning to walk down the hallway, Carlos followed me into my office. "Carlos, please sit down. You've been doing a great job around here keeping this station clean. I appreciate all your hard work. Antonio tells me you have been helping him out on your own with some recordings and keeping up the music library. I've heard your voice on a couple of spots and it's good. Antonio agrees. I know you have your small *leña* business, but I would like to offer you something new".

Reaching over to the intercom I called Carla. "Carla, find Antonio and send him in, *por favor.*" Carlos was all ears, and I could tell he was excited about what I was about to offer him.

"Good morning, *Jefe*," Antonio said as he walked in "Carlos, did he tell you yet?"

Before Carlos could answer, I said, "No, I haven't. I wanted you to be here with me, Antonio." I turned to Carlos and continued, "Carlos, Antonio and I want to offer you a job. A good-paying job and one of responsibility. Antonio needs your help in production, and, as you know, Marcos is leaving at the end of the year to go to the university up in Tegucigalpa.

"His night show needs to be filled, and we want you to train with him over the next few weeks to take over that show. We want you to work Mondays through Friday with Marcos from 7 to 11 p.m. and come in two hours earlier from 5 to 7 p.m. to do production and prepare for your show. We are going to put you on a weekly salary, including vacation pay, medical and dental. Carlos, we know you can do the job and we want you to start next Monday. I've hired another young man to take over your custodial jobs. How does that sound?"

"*Señor Tomás, Antonio, estoy muy satisfacho*. I am proud to say yes. I will do my best," Carlos said. We all stood and exchanged *abrazo*s.

After Carlos left, I asked Antonio, "You wanted to see me?"

"Everyone is worried about the military. We are getting a lot of phone calls. When those jets came in yesterday—coupled with the earthquake—it's making everyone nervous. I think we should do a little investigation on our own. We owe it to our listeners," said Antonio. "I get a strange feeling that something is about to happen. Maybe we should get someone in here to let us know what is going on out there . . . maybe Colonel Royale." "He's worthless and claims to know nothing," I told Antonio. "Besides I don't trust him."

"The base commander Perry isn't going to talk either," added Antonio.

"I'll second that," I said. "There must be a way to find out what those sensors are all about. They are popping up all over. I need to talk to Roberto. Maybe he can take a look at one of them and find out what they really are. Carla told me he wanted to see me . . . hold that thought." I reached the intercom again. "Carla, get Roberto in here for me."

I looked back to Antonio, "I've got an idea. What if I got Commander Perry to authorize some interviews with those young marines about how they like living here? You know: the food, the countryside, the entertainment and the flavor of Honduras. An outsider's view. Once you get to know them, then you could casually invite them to a night out. Dinner here in town and then the "*Vaquero*" for a little dancing and drinking with some of the local *señoritas*. You could take Carlos with you. Once they loosen up and start their youthful bragging, I'm sure you can get them to slip up on something interesting. I've never met a marine yet that didn't love to brag."

"I'll set it up for Saturday night. I'll call you Sunday morning to let you know what we find out, okay?" affirmed

Antonio.

"I'll be out of town this weekend so let's talk on Monday after I get back from breakfast at *El Rincon*," I said.

"Okay Thomas, when will you talk to the commander?" said Antonio.

"I'll call him this afternoon," I said.

The engineer walked in, "You wanted to see me, *Jefe*?"

"Perfect timing Roberto, sit down with us," I told him. "Antonio and I have been talking about those sensors that everyone is talking about —"

"That's just what I wanted to see you about, *Jefe*. One of my neighbors pulled one up that he found on his ranch and brought it over to my house yesterday. He wanted to know what it was. I took it apart last night and ran a few tests again this morning. It is a very sensitive listening device with a small transmitter attached," said Roberto.

"Is it a motion sensor too?" I asked.

"No, it is programmed to pick up high frequency sounds. It has nothing to do with motion sensing. Why do you ask, *Tomás*?" said Roberto.

"We've all been told that they are motion detectors to monitor the movements of the *narco traficantes*," injected Antonio.

"Well if all the rest are like the one I have, that would be impossible. These operate off a global positioning satellite using a triangulation theory to try and pinpoint the direction and exact position of a specific signal that is being emitted from somewhere on earth. It appears to me that they are picking up random frequencies, but they probably don't know precisely where they are coming from," said Roberto.

I said, "So, that is why they are moving around with those monitoring trucks, trying to pinpoint . . ."

Roberto jumped in, "What are you talking about—'monitoring trucks'?"

"We were told that the field troops were using monitoring trucks to listen to the sensor posts," said Antonio.

"They really don't need trucks. They can hear whatever they want off the satellite. They don't need trucks," emphasized Roberto.

"Antonio, this confirms our fears. Now we have to find out what is so damn important, that they would go to such lengths to cover up the real mission of their base at *La Semilla*," I said.

william clyde beadles

Chapter 4

"Commander Perry's office, Corporal Hanger speaking," said the corporal as he took my call.

"This is Thomas Clayton, is the Commander in?" I asked.

"Yes Sir. May I ask what your call is in reference to?" he said.

"The commander knows me. I am the owner of *Radio Onda* in town," I told him.

"Just a minute sir," He said and put me on hold.

"Thomas, how are you? Hope you're not calling about all that sensor nonsense," said Perry.

"Not really Cliff, but I've got an idea that might intrigue you. It's a story about how your men are enjoying their stay here in Honduras. What they like about the food, the customs, the girls," Cliff laughed. "You understand. An outsider's view. You know Cliff, it could help you with the negative image that is starting to build in the community. It will show the guys as real people who have respect and interest in our community," I told him.

"You're right, Thomas. That sounds like a great idea," said Cliff.

"I'll have my program director Antonio, you've met him before, call your office to set up the interviews. Whom should he contact at the base to make the arrangements?" I inquired.

"Have Antonio call Corporal Hanger. Hanger can organize it all for you," said Cliff.

I finished up some of my paperwork and decided to stop by the market and pick up some fresh-cut flowers for Amaya. I told her I would drop by after work for a drink and to discuss our weekend get-away. She worked so hard at *El Rincon*, and I basically just play. I enjoy every chance I have to get her out of the restaurant for a few days. On my way to the market, I called Antonio on his cell phone to let him know he needed to contact Corporal Hanger. I pulled up to the market and hopped out. The flower ladies bombarded me with special offers. I noticed some giant sunflowers and asked one of the flower ladies to put together a long-stem bouquet of sunflowers and mixed colored flowers. I told her to think of the sun, surrounded by a bright rainbow of colors. She got the idea and I had an armful of beautiful flowers for Amaya.

I continued on to *El Rincon*. As I passed by the *Iglesia*, I noticed *Padre Jesus* talking with Profe in front of Robin's shop. Profe is what everyone called him. I never did know his real name. He was always trying to teach the kids English, so he received the title as the 'Walking Professor of English', or "Profe," for short. Profe pushed his ice cream cart all over town, his bells ringing to let everyone know he was there.

"Profe, has *Señora* Hoggan ever painted you?" asked *Padre Jesus.*

"*No, Padre solo mi tio Ernesto,*" said Profe. "*Pero el se murio hace mas de viente años.*"

"You mean to tell me she painted your uncle who died more than 20 years ago?" asked the stunned Priest.

"*Sí, Padre,* he was standing in the crowd of one of her paintings she had in her window last summer," said Profe. "If you look closely at the people in her paintings, you might even see someone you know that has passed away. *Señora* Hoggan has a gift. She sees people that aren't here. See this one of the *señoras* selling flowers? Look at the two ladies sitting next to them with their baskets of vegetables. Just a little while ago, I sold some ice cream to a *señora* that said the two women were relatives of hers who died 10 years ago. Every time *Señora* Hoggan puts out some new paintings, everyone comes by to see if they can identify one of their ancestors."

"When did you first notice this, Profe?" asked *Padre Jesus.*

"It was about three years ago when *la familia* Hoggan first moved here. I heard people talking among themselves about her paintings. I have looked at every new one since then, but I have only seen my *Tio* Ernesto. But many people around here have seen a lot of familiar faces," said Profe.

"Has anyone asked *Señora* Hoggan about the people in her painting? You know, like, how does she come up with those faces?" asked *Padre Jesus.*

Profe said, "No one wants to ask her. They believe she has a gift, and people want to see their past relatives. They are afraid that if they tell her what she is doing, she might lose her gift."

Just then two ladies and three small kids came walking by the shop. They asked Profe for ice cream for the kids who sat down in front of the shop to eat while the two women went in to look at Robin's new paintings.

I pulled up in front of the *Rincon* and walked in with my flower rainbow. *Don Pepe* was there to greet me. He pointed to the flowers as I walked past.

"Somebody get lucky tonight, *Sí, Señor*," Pepe said to himself as I walked directly to the bar. It was a little early, so only a few people were at the dinner tables. The bar was virtually empty, with only one couple looking like tourists sitting at the end of the bar. I set the flowers on the barstool next to me and told Ignacio to bring me a beer.

"*Un momento*, Ignacio," I called out. "I've changed my mind. Bring me two *Coco Locos*."

"Yes sir, *Don Tomás*," Ignacio said and went straight to work on my drinks. I stretched and looked around to see if anyone was still here from lunch, but there appeared to be just the tourists.

"Here you are, Don *Tomás*," said Ignacio, as he set his chilled coconut drinks in front of me. And with one of his funny faces, he said, "Why two? Special occasion?" He leaned over the bar to peek at the flowers.

"Wipe that silly grin off your face and go tell your boss that there are two "*Locos*" at the bar and they need some help," I said grinning myself.

Amaya came out from the back all-serious but when

she saw me at the front of the house, she broke into a girly smile. With a very coquettish walk, she moved down the bar straight for me. Putting her elbows on the bar, she looked across at me and said, "I see one loco here—where is the other one?"

"She just got here," I teased.

She leaned across the bar to kiss me and stopped when she saw the flowers on the chair next to me. I scooped them up and handed them to Amaya.

"You're the sunshine at the end of my rainbow," I told her.

"Oooh, Thomas, they are beautiful," she said and walked around the bar and put the flowers back on the barstool from where I took them. She put her arms around my neck and gave me a great big kiss. She turned just as quickly and picked up the flowers again, set them on the bar and sat down in their place.

"*Tomás*, you are the sweetest, the most *dulce!*" She gave me that look and turned to sip her *Coco Loco*. "I don't know what is more loco—the coconut or you," She smiled.

"Honey, everything is set for this weekend," I said. "We can leave first thing Friday morning. With everything that is going on around here, I think we need a break. I am looking forward to pure relaxation. Just you. Just me . . . and . . ."

"And LaLa Land!" laughed Amaya. "How about some snacks before you have to go? Yes?"

"Sounds good to me! What do you have in mind?" I teased again.

"Ignacio, *triganos un plato!*" she called out.

william clyde beadles

CHAPTER 5

"*Tomás* more *jugo?*" Tida asked.

"Thank you, yes. What have you packed for our lunch today?" I asked. I told Scott I would bring the lunch out to his site at *Xhutlan*.

"You have sandwich *de jamon y queso* with *lechuga, tomates y* onion just the way you like it. I made potato chips last night because I know Don Scott *le gusta* and I made an *ensalada de frutas* with cookies for a dessert. They are all in the Coleman, along with a bag of ice and sodas," said Tida.

"What would I do without you, Tida?" I told her.

She turned and walked away saying, "I'd tell you but you wouldn't believe me."

She was probably right. She really does take care of everything around here. I'm lucky to have such a good woman. She's honest, hardworking and thinks of everything. She'd been after me already to get everything together for my Friday get-away with Amaya. I know I keep telling her I'll do it. But she knows as well as I do, that it won't get done unless she does it. And she will. When I come home on Thursday, it will all be laid out on my bed. If I want to get in that bed, I'll have to agree with the choices that she laid out and pack them. It's either do it, or sleep on the floor.

I picked up the cooler and put it in the back of my truck. My dog "Bark" had been watching my every move from under the mango tree. He was just a pup when I brought him down with me from the states. He's a border collie, black and white, with one brown eye and one blue. He loves everyone. Ever since he was young, he rarely ever barked, so I named him, "Bark". He has natural inborn herding instincts. He loves to herd the ducks around, and when I take him out to Scott's, he can't wait to keep the cattle rounded up. He darts back and forth, with his head to the ground, his butt in the air. His concentration is amazing. His eyes and head act as one to stare down his subjects. I say subjects and not prey because he thinks he is the Lord of the Flock and establishes very quickly that he is in control. He has incredible patience. He was herding butterflies as a puppy.

"Bark." His ears pricked up pulling his head and eyes up with them, "Want to go for a ride?" I asked him.

He was waiting for the invitation. Jumping to his feet, he was right beside me.

"Up," I said and he launched himself into the truck and over to the back seat, which I had folded down, so he could get easily from one side of the truck to the other. He loved to go for a ride.

Bark and I were on our way. We quickly scooted through town, out to the Pan American. About 10 minutes up the road, I took the cutoff to San Rafael. At the next junction, I took a right until the road came to an end. From there, it was just a dirt road that led into the jungle. Bark, with his head poking through the passenger side window of the truck, was sniffing out every new smell. Bark has a sense of smell and hearing that is hundreds of times more broad and sensitive than mine. I've often wondered what pictures go through his brain as he picks up a strange or different scent. Can Bark use his sense of smell to see visual pictures in his mind? Familiar food smells for one can conjure up memories from my past, like images of Thanksgiving with pumpkin pie; plumeria blossoms and a cute blonde on a warm night in Aina Haina; or the smell on your clothes after a long flight, the fragrance of *odour d' Boeing* . We humans have a lot to learn. Not just from dogs, but everything. They say we only use a small percentage of our brains. I've always been intrigued by man's self-imposed limitations and his potential to break free from them.

As I came out of the jungle into the clearing at the meadows of *Xhutlan*, I felt like I had just traversed a portal in time. The earthen mounds and partially uncovered buildings of this small Mayan site held many secrets. Scott was hoping to find the answer to some of them. I looked across the meadow to the other side and saw the Temple of *K'in*. Scott's truck was parked along side two other trucks that had carried his workers. They were busy on another building. I saw Scott by the entrance to the temple, giving instructions to three of his men. I pulled up under a shade tree and Bark and I got out.

"Hi, Scott," I shouted.

"Hey Bark, come here boy!" Scott yelled back.

Bark's ears perked up and, with tail wagging, ran directly over to Scott. Bark stopped and sat down right in from of him to retrieve his reward—a pat on his head and a couple of rubs, "Good boy, Bark. Hi, Thomas," said Scott.

Bark ran back to me as I approached Scott. "Go ahead Bark, look around boy. Go on," I said. Bark, with his nose to the ground, set off to explore on his own.

"You have uncovered a lot since the last time I was here," I told Scott.

The meadows of *Xhutlan* were discovered quite a few years ago, but no one had ever touched them. Authorities knew of the mounds and ruins, but with all of the thousands of sites in Honduras many like *Xhutlan* have gone untouched. It is believed that the inhabitants were the *Chorotega* Indians, but Scott told me that the *Chorotegas* were more recent arrivals, probably around 700 to 1000 A.D. The Mayans predate them by several thousand years. There are several other sites around Choluteca that have been looted and/or explored, but this site has been untouched. Untouched for perhaps three or four thousand years! The other sites in this southern part of Honduras showed signs of a mixture of Mayan and Inca civilizations. Scott's theory is that this area was a cross over area of the two cultures. The South American Incas were trading as far north as Central America and the Mayans and Aztecs as far south as Central America. The over lapping trade area connected the two major civilizations of that time. *Xhutlan* was a small village with just one temple dedicated to the Sun God, *K'in*.

"Thomas, let's go for a walk around the temple. I would like you to get a feel for the outside dimensions before we go in," said Scott.

As we walked around the outside perimeter, I was not very impressed as it wasn't a very large structure above the ground. When I was at Scott's party last Sunday, he told me a lot of the structure was actually below the surface. Scott told me what he found interesting was that the Mayans built such an elaborate temple so far south of the center of the Mayan civilization. Most learned men believe that the first Mayans began their history in southern Mexico, and then moved southward to Central Honduras and El Salvador. Scott had told me he believed just the reverse. He believed the first Mayan city was somewhere in this area. The first Mayans tried to travel south into Nicaragua, but the land was too arid. So they went north and found fertile lands, plentiful game and mountains full of timber and minerals. A few outposts are scattered here in the southern part of Honduras, but they are dated toward the end of the height of the ancient Mayan civilization. This site didn't fit the same time period of all the rest in the Choluteca region.

Coming back around to the entrance, Scott said, "What intrigues me most about this site is that it doesn't fit. It's like the myth of *Ciudad Blanca*. For more than 50 years pilots have seen from the air a white city in the jungle that seems to appear and disappear. No one has actually pinpointed its location, and sometimes years will go by and no one will see it at all. The majority of the sightings have been from the province of *Gracias a Dios*. The more recent sightings have placed Ciudad Blanca closer to this area in the Province of Choluteca than *Gracias a Dios*. No one has ever been able to find *Ciudad Blanca* or prove if it actually exists. The jungle goes through cycles of wet and dry. Along with that comes times of heavy tropical growth with the jungle canopies and vegetation covering everything up. Then come periods of drought when the jungle recedes or burns. Many new sites are discovered during such times from the air. *Ciudad Blanca*, though, has escaped all attempts to locate it. I know this site is not *Ciudad Blanca*, but it, too, is elusive and mysterious. There is only this one temple. And it has been designed to hide itself from the world. The scattered remains of other buildings appear to have been from workers who lived here, protecting it almost like guards. Where they went and why this site was abandoned is a mystery. Why was this single temple built here and abandoned? It doesn't fit the general concept of cities that are common to other Mayan areas. It's not even a city. It's almost like an outpost or a monument . . . no, it's more like a visitors' center to a national park."

At that exact moment, I felt a rush of goose bumps flash over my body. "Scott, I just felt something."

"Did it give you a rush or goose bumps?" Scott said with a little excitement in his voice.

"Yes. It shot up and down my spine—you know, like when something hits you. I mean *really* hits you. When you come to the realization of something very important or surprising," I said.

"Go with your feelings," Scott said. "I knew you were the

right person to help me."

This caught me off guard, I'm not prone to a lot of what I call sci-fi crap, but I know I have a spiritual interest, especially when it comes to people. I've seen too much in my life not to have a feeling for something beyond three dimensions, as we know it.

"Scott what do these symbols mean over the archway? Didn't I see them in Robin's painting of you?" I asked.

"You're right. Exactly over the arch is *K'in* the sun God who is the beginning of all things. Going down the left side of the entrance are the symbols of life. The symbols on the right are the underworld and the afterlife. If this was the entrance to a museum, I would say that the entrance tells the story of the Mayan life cycle we are in now. Let's go inside," said Scott. "Watch your head."

The entrance was five feet across and little more than five feet high. We ducked inside. I immediately felt the coolness as we stepped out of the sunlight. Scott had lined the interior with overhead fluorescent lights. He had a 950-amp generator to power the lights and equipment needed to run the site. It also powered the supply tent and the living quarters for the security that patrolled the site from looters.

"This is the main room, just the way I found it," Scott said, as he walked to a carved rock table in the middle of the chamber. The room almost felt like a reception area. Two smaller rooms went off to each side and I could see behind the stone table the entrance to the great pyramid chamber that Scott had just opened.

Scott continued, "The entrance to the temple did not have

a door when I discovered this place. It has been sealed shut for hundreds of years. Look at the walls. Over the centuries, the jungle's damp humid conditions have slowly destroyed the colors on the wall murals. Fungus and moss have eaten away at the walls, too. Only the carvings on the table here are still intact. They tell the story of the creation myth and the beginning of the life cycle. It is the cosmogenesis, or, the origin of the world. The top of the table seems to be a universe map showing our earth here in its relationship to the Sun, Venus, Mars and Jupiter. Over here are the Milky Way and some of the constellations that are seen in Mayan mythology.

Remember what I told you about the end of the cycle? The end of one cycle is the birth of another. All of the truths and facts of this cycle will expire and a new phase or cycle of growth will take over. We are on the edge of something very dramatic. Now look over here: this portal was sealed off. Hidden on purpose. I was using a sonar device on the walls, when I discovered that on this wall there appeared to be an opening behind it. I made a couple of simple probes and bingo!—there it was. It took us a week to open the wall to how you see it now."

"What's in there?" I asked.

"I really don't want to tell you. I want you to experience it like I did for the first time. Grab a hard hat and flip on the headlamp. Here's your lantern," Scott said.

"Wait a minute. You want me to go in there alone? I was half kidding about being afraid of the dark, but now I think I am." I looked at the silence on his face and continued, "You really want me to go in there alone, don't you?"

"Thomas, remember I told you about missing something?" Scott said.

"Yeah," I said, nodding my head.

"Well, I want you to see, hear and feel what I first did. Now just relax. There's nothing in there that will kill you—I don't think," said Scott, with that devilish, child-like look on his face.

"You don't think!" I exclaimed.

"No, really. Just go in and let that spiritual side of you loose. Don't hold back. Allow the experience to soak in. When you're ready, call me and I will come in," Scott said.

I looked at the door and then back at him. Grabbing the lantern from his hand, I turned and walked into the opening, venturing in about 10 or 12 feet to discover the steps that led down into the chamber. There was a tightness in my stomach. It was a mixture of fear and anticipation. Slightly bent over as I walked, my hard hat hit the ceiling once before making my first step down. With my second step, I was clear of the tunnel's ceiling and stood up straight. Holding the lantern up I saw the chamber for the first time, but only parts of it as the light of the lantern couldn't reveal the room. The first thing I noticed was color. The colors were brilliant, not faded away like those exposed to the elements outside and in the entrance area. It was so quiet. I could hear my breathing, as the feeling of fear and anxiety disappear. The excitement of discovery filled the void. Slowly I descended to the main floor where there was a large boulder towering over me. I walked over to one wall and touched it just to make sure it was real. It was. I couldn't get over how brilliant the colors were. I did sense a noise in my ears. I could feel the noise, but I couldn't hear it. I *thought* I could hear it, but really couldn't. I was confused. It was a sensation of sound like having the speakers off, with no sound coming out but still feeling the vibrations. These vibrations were soft and very calming. I called out to Scott to come down.

As he walked down the steps, I met him at the bottom. "Scott, this is . . . this is just too much for words. And, Scott, I can feel something."

"Let's climb up on the platform atop the boulder. I've got a surprise for you," Scott said. "Leave the lanterns here; we'll get them on the way down."

Setting the lanterns aside, we climbed the boulder, using the carved steps and hand holds with just our helmet lamps for light. When we reached the top, Scott told me to face the north wall. He grabbed his radio and called his foreman, "Raul, hit the lights."

Scott had placed metal tree stands of lights around the room, along with fluorescent lighting. The room exploded with light and I saw the great mural on the inner façade of the north wall. I was overwhelmed with the magnitude of the frescos, the detail and the colors. The sheer beauty was overwhelming. What did it all mean? Who created all this? And more importantly, why? I slowly turned around to take in the entire room and finally looked back at Scott.

He had a very proud look on his face. "Thomas, if this is what I think it is, we are getting a look into the future of the next cycle," Scott said.

"You mean the one that comes after the one we are in

now? The one that is supposed to start in a couple of weeks?"
I blurted out.

"Exactly. The stone table at the entrance tells the story of
the fourth cycle. It shows the Mayan end date of this winter solstice, when the sun will be in a rare alignment with
the Galactic Center, the center of the universe. The Mayan
end date is December 21, 2012—as you said: in about two
weeks. Thomas, if I am right, we are about to experience
the end of the world, as we know it, and the birth of a new
one. This chamber represents the new one, the fifth cycle in
the Mayan calendar. The wall mural begins with the rebirth
and spells out the promises that come with it. There is nothing anywhere in the world that even comes close to what is
explained in this chamber. We are running out of time. If
only we could figure out the whole meaning of this mural,
we might be able to do something! What? I don't know,"
Scott said.

We both pondered that thought for a minute, and then I
said, "Maybe we aren't expected to do anything. Maybe we
are here to record what we see. What we hear. What we feel.
Maybe in two weeks we won't even be here."

"I have been able to decipher part of the mural.
Unfortunately, some of the mural has been damaged so
there are some gaps," Scott said, as he started to point out
what he had learned so far. "Just before the upcoming end
date, and the beginning or the rebirth, it appears those living will experience great calamities with storms, volcanoes
erupting and earthquakes. The earth opens up and the living and the dead of the underworld unite and together they

walk into the Sun, their God *K'in*. They are consumed in the power of *K'in*, or the fire, but they emerge together, apparently unharmed. Then, they enter into, the best way I can explain it, a box that appears to be floating. See here? I'm not sure why it is floating. Maybe it's not. I'm not sure yet. The Mayan symbol for the earth appears, here under the box. It also appears in front of the sun symbol and the earth symbol again appears inside of the sun. See the drawing up there? That has me puzzled. They enter the box in two streams and exit the other side single file. Then they expand out to this representation of a crowd or multitude. Now look at this —"

"That's a work of art! What are those stones around the circle?" I said in amazement, interrupting Scott.

"What you are seeing is some kind of time device or clock. Around the circle there are jewels of every kind. Some of them, I should say most of them, as far as we know didn't even exist during the early Mayan years. Some of the stones I'm not sure I have ever seen before. They each have a different shade of color. On one side of the circle, they begin with a dark, rich intensity of purple and progress through the color spectrum to a pure, white crystal represented by that diamond, and at the bottom it then reverses the saturation to fill in the other half of the circle. There it begins with a light gray jewel and grows in blackness to the top of the halfway point, then its intensity fades back into the colored jewels again on the other side. What is puzzling here is each jewel is numbered."

"But the symbol by each jewel is the same symbol as the one next to it. What's that all about?" I asked.

"That's one of the things that I haven't figured out yet. Each symbol is the same. And that symbol is the mathematical representation of the Mayan 'zero'. It doesn't make sense. Every jewel is different, yet each one is represented as zero. Maybe I'm too close to it. That's why I have you along, my good friend. Maybe you will see something that I don't," said Scott.

"It's so beautiful. Can we go down and take a closer look?" I asked.

"Let's finish up here first. I want you to get the whole overview before we start to take it apart piece-by-piece," Scott said, as he continued. "The next one has me equally puzzled. It has something to do with thinking, or communication, or writing. Again, I am at a loss. The next one is the center point of the mural. It shows a tree. And yes, it is made of gold and inlaid with seashells for leaves. In the roots of the tree are a myriad, of small symbols. Look straight up the main trunk to the top of the mural. See those four symbols? One is the father of all fathers. The other three symbols are each different, but they all represent important men. The next mural appears to me as a 3D type of map showing our earth and its position in the skies in relation to our solar system and then the entire universe. The next three are really fascinating. The first one shows what appears to be a conference of important people, but all of them are also identified as Gods. The next area—don't laugh—looks like a zoo. But as you can see, they are not animals or birds or fish, as we know them. They don't exist anywhere on earth that I'm aware of."

"Look at that one. It has hundreds of eyes and the body

of a snake. I think someone was dipping into some mountain mushrooms, when they came up with that one," I said jokingly.

"This last one looks like a brain, with bolts of lightning shooting out of it. The brain is made from different chips of jade and the lightning bolts are inlaid gold. The end of the mural has a monolith that protrudes from the wall at an angle, jutting six feet into the chamber. It is made of some dark black alloy that has been cut and polished on the front and remains rough and pitted on the back. I tried to make a scratch to get a piece to sample, but I couldn't mar it. It's eerie because the only reflection is just of you as if nothing else around you or behind you exists. You can see through the reflected image to the background, as if your reflection was a ghost or spirit. The background seems to go on forever, much like the reflection of a mirror in a mirror. You'll see when we go down. I have no explanation for it," Scott said.

Just then we both heard a rumbling from above us. Immediately, I thought of an earthquake.

"Don't worry, Thomas; thunder. The afternoon storm is coming a little bit early today. I've heard it down here before, usually in the late afternoon. It has the muffled sound of an earthquake, but I assure you it is thunder. *Chak*, the Mayan God of Rain and Lightning, is just paying us an early visit," Scott reassured me. Immediately, there was another crash of thunder, only this one seemed a lot closer, judging by its volume.

We both heard footsteps behind coming from above us near the chamber entrance. I should correct myself: paw steps. Evidently, Bark had enough of the lightning and thunder and decided to come in out of the rain. He stopped in his tracks and looked at us. I whistled for him to come, and he bounded down the steps to the floor below us. We climbed down from the rock platform in the middle of the room and he seemed happy to see us. The thunder made Bark a little nervous.

We started at the beginning of the mural and proceeded along it to the end. As we walked in front of the black monolith, I saw what Scott was talking about. I saw my own reflection, Scott's, and even Bark's. Yet I could not see any other details of the room behind us in the reflections. It was as if it could only read us. It dawned on me: maybe it could only reflect life and not reflect non-life forms. It was an eerie feeling. As I looked past my reflection, I could see inside the rock what looked like the universe, with tiny pinpoints of light extending to what appeared as endless.

I moved behind Scott, but only the parts of my body that were on either side of him appeared in the reflection. His reflection blocked parts of my reflection the same as a mirror would. Bark seemed confused. He saw another dog and us in the reflection. The hair bristled on his collar, and he slowly walked toward his reflection. Every move he made, the other dog mimicked in the reflection. His herding instincts kicked in and his reflection followed his every move. He quickly backed up two steps and moved to his left. His reflection followed. He straightened up, and with a puzzled look on his face, looked to me then back at the other dog. I reached down and stroked him on the head and said, "It's okay, boy;

good boy Bark."

"This is incredible. Simply incredible. It seems like it is electronic or something. What is it?" I asked.

"Come around and look at the backside with me. It is pocked just like a meteorite. I've seen them cut open, before and they have the same shiny appearance once they have been polished. But the ones I have seen function just like mirrors. You can see everything in the reflection but you don't see the endless inside of the meteorite like this one.

Judging on the size of this, it must weight close to 200 tons. The largest one on display is 32 tons and is in the American Museum of Natural History in New York City. The largest one ever found was in Africa and is estimated to weigh 60 tons. Meteorites are mostly iron, a small percentage of nickel and traces of other metals like cobalt and some metals that do not even exist on earth. Some have a mixture of silicates in them, which could account for the pinpoints of light, but they don't glow like the ones on the front of this one do. How this got here I don't have the foggiest. The Maya didn't have the technology to cut and polish a meteorite . . . Okay that's it for today's tour. Now where's that lunch you promised me?" Scott said, rubbing his stomach. "In the truck. Let's go get it. I'm hungry, too."

"First, I need to look at something and then we can go," Scott said as he walked over to a table he has set up with his documents and drawings scrawled all over its top.

"Okay," I answered back.

I took that opportunity to go back to the monolith or meteorite to take one more look at it. It was as if it was calling me.

Alone, this time I gazed at my reflection. It appeared different from just a few minutes ago. The image I saw almost didn't seem human, but it still looked like me ... yet it had an eerie luminosity, a soft glow or brightness to it that was somewhat surreal. My reflected image was translucent, more like a ghostly image than a solid physical identical likeness. I had the impression that I was looking at my soul. Not my body; my soul. I felt the sweat running down the back of my neck and a weakness in my stomach. Adrenaline pumped through my veins like jet fuel. Frightened, terrified and confused all at the same time, I suddenly realized it must be my soul! But if this was my soul what did it want with me. Was my soul here to retrieve me—beckoning me to follow its image into the rock and leave this life for some other? Standing there, I knew I had arrived at a pivotal point in my life. Was life confronting me or challenging me?

Although a confrontation with death didn't feel eminent, I knew I was staring it in the face. The more I studied the image, the more uncomfortable and terrified I became. I felt physically paralyzed. For what seemed an eternity, yet was probably only seconds, nothing moved. We were frozen in a standoff. I finally pulled together enough courage to reach out and touch the rock just to prove to myself that it was just a reflection. Mentally I prepared to make the first move and assure myself that my mind was just playing games with me. I reached out to touch the image, and it responded. It moved as I moved in a mirror-like reverse motion. I started to regain my composure and confidence as the reflection moved exactly like a reflection should. As our fingers slowly moved toward each other's approaching the mirror-like surface, I expected they would come to a stop when we 'touched.' To my surprise, they didn't. Our fingers *actually* touched. Stunned, I looked up into the face of the image and I saw my reflection smile back at me, but I was not smiling. I was too frightened at that moment to smile. As I looked into its eyes, I felt its hand grasp me around the wrist. As mine coupled his, I quickly looked down. I was holding onto myself in another world, another time, another place. With my arm half in the rock and half out, I looked back to the eyes. I had forgotten to breathe. I sucked in a deep breath, continued to stare deep into the eyes of my soul. I sensed I was being offered an option, a choice: I could continue on into the rock to join my soul to perhaps another life or stay and see what was still in store for me on this earth. My mind raced. I knew that if I chose to stay, it would not be without its consequences. I wasn't ready to move into the next dimension of life's progression, whatever it might be. I had just made a major decision to change my life by coming to Choluteca, to stay in one place, to find meaning to my life. That was why I was here. I was tired of running all over the world. I wasn't ready to travel to a new place. I had made my decision to stop running. I didn't want to chase another story. Yet, maybe this was part of that 'great story' I had always been searching for, maybe I was supposed to go. Or perhaps, I wasn't supposed to find the story ... it was supposed to find me.

As I let go of my image and backed away from the rock

my reflection watched. I knew that I had received a glimpse into the future. Almost like a vision that had no visuals, a voice that had no sound; an understanding came to me. I sensed that the original concept of the millennium was still alive.

The millennium we all knew, with all of its predictions, had come and gone. For some it was a great relief, for others it was a disappointment. With in weeks it was old news and life went on. The end of the world was yet another media hyped event that turned out to be all hype and no substance. What I was soon to learn was time on this earth was still rapidly counting down to a dramatic climax, yet no one knew it. The secret was right here in this ancient Mayan Temple. The millennium hadn't missed us; it was still staring us straight in the face. The world was just using the wrong calendar.

Not exactly sure of what I had just experienced, I decided not to reveal this to Scott right away. I needed a little more time to decipher it all and how I felt about it.

We climbed out of the chamber with Bark taking the lead. Reaching the top, we ducked down and walked through the tunnel to the entrance room. I could still hear the rain outside. "We're going to get wet, boy," I said to Bark.

"Let's go over to my office. We'd better run for it," Scott said.

"I've got to get the lunch out of my truck first," I told Scott. "Take Bark with you."

Bark and Scott ran off to the shelter of Scott's office and I jumped into my truck, deciding to drive it over to the front of his building. I got out and pulled the food and the Coleman from the back of the truck. I laid it out on the table that was under the overhang of his building.

"Hey, this is quite a spread, Thomas. Looks like Tida didn't forget me either—her famous potato chips!" Scott exclaimed.

I bit into my first sandwich and pondered for a second while I chewed. We had a bit of a conflict here. We could be sitting on one of the most exciting stories of our time, maybe of all time, even if Scott was only half-right. That monolith alone was beyond explanation. Bark curled up next to my feet and fell into a deep siesta. I wondered what was going through Scott's mind. He was quiet and pensive as he ate. We had a lot to digest in a very short time—and not just lunch. Scott worked like an archeologist at a snail's pace, literally turned over every stone as he methodically attempted to piece together the whole picture from history. However, I'm sure Scott thought everything was going too fast. As a journalist working with short deadlines, sometimes interpreting a story live as it happens, it wasn't going slow enough for me. Everything was developing at a speed that I was actually uncomfortable with. Deadlines are deadlines, but the possible end of the world was a little more of a "deadline" than I was willing to cope with right now.

"Scott," I said.

"Thomas," Scott said at the exact same time.

We both sat back and started laughing. "Are you thinking what I'm thinking?"

"Thomas, the only people to set foot in that chamber since it was sealed has been you, me, Raul and two of my best workers," Scott said.

"And Bark," I said with a chuckle.

"In less than two weeks, if I am right, something very big is going to happen. Like I said before, we may not be able to do anything. Maybe we are not supposed to do anything to upset what is about to occur. I have protected this so far because I'm afraid that we have stumbled onto something we were not supposed to find. Remember, I said that this temple is out of place and appears to have been built specifically to be hidden. It is instructional—almost like a visitors' center. I told you I needed your help. So what do you think?" Scott asked.

Not ready to totally open up to Scott as to what I had felt and experienced when I looked at my reflection, I focused my comments toward the elaborate time piece made of stone and gems, "I keep thinking about that round clock or calendar or whatever it is. The stones have me fascinated. You said that the symbols around the outside of the circle were all representations of 'zero.' So what if I was on the other side of the world and you were still here. We would be in the same time but in different places. We could talk to each other by phone in the same time. The Mayan round clock would say it is 'zero' time where I was and: 'zero' time here where you are. By Mayan time it would be the same time, but the way we tell time, it would be a different time. Or should I say a difference in time. Now if I were to fly around the world to where you are now, you would have to wait some time to see me, but if you go around on the Mayan clock, it would say that the time was still the same—'zero.' Maybe it is a dimension that we don't know yet. Stay with me Scott! Maybe, just maybe, it is trying to tell us that I could move from one place to another and no, or 'zero' time, would elapse. Think of it. I could be in two places in the blink of an eye . . . not even that. You know, 'Beam me up, Scotty' stuff," I said.

Scott laughed. We continued for a couple more hours, talking over ideas and looking at pictures and drawings that Scott had made of the chamber. The rain stopped, the sun set, the sky was fading quickly, and the almost full moon was just coming up.

Bark got up and went out for a pee. As I turned to see if Bark finished his duty tour, he ran back toward us, stopped dead in his tracks, did an about face with his ears perked up, then turned his head to follow something that he heard.

"Did you just hear something?" I asked Scott.

"No, did you?" Scott replied.

"No, me either, but Bark is picking something up," I said, getting to my feet.

"It can't be from any of the men, because they are all in the back fixing their dinner. They haven't started their rounds yet," Scott said.

We walked a few steps off the porch to see if we could spot anything.

Bark hunched down and started to herd something. He ran back and forth, his head and eyes following whatever he was hearing. We still didn't see anything. Bark wouldn't give up as he herded something we couldn't see. Just then the security night lights popped on startling me.

"Don't worry. It's just the night lights kicking on. They're on a timer," Scott reassured.

Bark was now about 50 yards away, still in his herding mode. I'd never seen him do anything like this before, but I'd seen a lot of things today that I had never seen before. All of a sudden, he stopped and sat. He acted like someone was petting him, but no one was there. He looked back at Scott and me, then back toward the edge of the clearing. I followed his eyes and spotted what looked like a small kid in the darkness walking into the jungle.

"Look!" I shouted to Scott pointing to the edge of the meadow where the jungle began.

"What? What?" Scott replied.

"Didn't you see him? It looked like a young Indian boy walking into the trees and disappearing."

Bark loped back toward us, his tail wagging like he had just been out to play with a friend. He didn't seem spooked. He was very content.

"No, I didn't see him, but I think I should add some additional security around here," Scott said. "Thomas, let's go in and talk about this for a few more minutes."

As we turned to walk back, out of the corner of my eye I caught a glimpse of light, a twinkle in the sky.

"Damn, look over there!" I said quickly.

Hovering in the silent mode was an F-1000 fighter, the twilight of the moon bouncing off its black skin. It looked like it was monitoring what we were doing. It silently moved straight up into the cloud cover and disappeared.

We both looked at each other and then walked back under the porch area. Scott yelled to Raul to send the guards out early and to go over near where I saw the boy and look around.

"Thomas, I think the military is looking for something, too," Scott said as he sat down.

"I agree, but I don't know what. I also agree that, for now, we have to protect this from everyone else since we still are not sure what we are dealing with. What irony! You may have discovered the most important archeological find in the history of this world, plus I am sitting on the greatest story to come down the pike, not just for this world but maybe for the next, and neither one of us can tell anyone about it. The monolith alone is a story unto itself. If that were to get out, we would be swamped with reporters, military, governments, religious people and the normal 10,000 crazies, not to mention tourists! We can't tell anyone. We have to protect this for now. I'm not sure exactly why we should. I just know we should. Do you agree?" I asked.

"You are feeling and thinking just like me. Maybe we were twins in a different life. Who knows—maybe we will be in the next life," Scott said with a chuckle. "I knew I could count on you, my friend. Thanks," Scott reassured me. "And, yes, I agree!"

"Come on, Bark, let's go."

CHAPTER 6

Robin's artistic gift was not her only gift. What Profe had explained to *Padre Jesus* about her painting past relatives of the people of Choluteca proved to be a pivotal point in learning what was about to happen to all of us.

Scott still had not figured out what Robin's paintings really held, and I was still in the dark too. It wouldn't be until later that we would both understand the significance of Robin's visit to her daughter's school. Little did we know then that a small boy—an on-looker like us—would be captured by Robin's imagination and end up in her next painting. It was this small boy who soon would reveal himself to all of us. For then, he was just a small, insignificant local child, a simple face in the background, simply a blend of reality and imagination.

Robin pulled up next to the schoolyard fence and parked her Land Rover. It was ten in the morning and filtered sunlight cascaded, penetrating the trees surrounding the soccer field, falling cathedral-like upon the grassy field, where the children were busy with their morning recess. Little Lori in her soccer shorts ran along with her classmates after the small black and white *pelota*.

Robin got out and walked to the back, reached for her camera case, took out two Nikons, loaded them. She picked up her 300mm Nikkor lens mounting it on the first body. Snapping into place her 80-210mm Nikkor Zoom lens and walking up close to the rod iron fence near a hedge of brilliant orange and purple bougainvillea, she began to take pictures of Lori at play. The motor drive on the Nikon hummed quietly as she worked her way unnoticed down the fence in one direction and then followed as the play on the field shifted from one end to the other. From these shots of Lori, running free in the sunlight with her spirits high, Robin would do her magic, turning them into a wonderful painting that she would present to Lori for Christmas. Robin and Scott really didn't know how much longer they would be able to see her in such bliss. The beginning signs of her sickness were now starting to show. Eventually the painting would be a memory of Lori's short but beautiful life on this earth.

On the opposite side of the playing field from Robin, in the shadows of the tall mangroves, was another small child. He was outside the fence, looking in upon the children at play. To Robin, he went unnoticed. Her focus was intently on Lori. When she had finished her last picture, she returned to the Land Rover and carefully placed her cameras back into their cases. She started toward the driver's side of the Land Rover and stopped. She turned around, compelled to take one last look at Lori at play before she returned to her studio to develop her film. Lori was still in the game and had not noticed Robin near the fence. Without her cameras, Robin simply watched her child at play as any mother would. The bell rang, ending the recess period, and all the children ran back to the building. Robin stood for a minute after all the children had gone and stared at the empty field.

Later that day, Robin selected the prints she wanted in her darkroom. She preferred film over digital systems. Digital cameras, with all of their advancements in recent years, still could not capture the pure essence of light that film could. Robin could control her cameras almost as if they were brushes in her hands. Over the years, she had developed her own technique and style with her cameras and in the darkroom. After the prints came out of the dryer, she selected a few that she would use to be the basis of her painting of Lori at play in the schoolyard. She came out of the darkroom and spread them on her cutting table in her studio. While she was pondering them, she munched on an apple. It was almost time to go pick up the kids from school. She gathered up the three she made as her final selection and walked out of the studio into the gallery. She had her handcrafted, leather satchel slung over her shoulder that the leather maker had made for her at *El Mercado Merced*.

Silvia, Robin's sales girl, was busy with a customer, but noticed Robin as she walked quickly through the gallery, pointing to the watch on her hand and then, with a wave goodbye, was out the door. Silvia knew that it meant Robin was off for the day and would be headed to the school for the kids.

Standing in front of her shop was *Padre Jesus*, consoling an older woman dressed all in black. They were both looking at Robin's painting of the little girl at her first communion. The woman was softly weeping. *Padre Jesus*, with his arm around the woman in black was gently speaking to her.

"Is everything all right, Father?" Robin inquired, with concern at the fact that they were both looking at her painting.

"Everything is just fine, *Señora* Hoggan. She is just touched by the beauty of your painting," *Padre Jesus* replied.

"Are you sure?" Robin asked.

"Yes, I am sure. Everything is okay."

Robin nodded her understanding that all was well, but she was not totally convinced, maybe because what she didn't know was that *Padre Jesus* wasn't exactly clear as to what he told Robin. Yes, the painting touched the woman. But what was concerning the old woman was the fact that she could see her mother—sitting in the second row of the church— who passed away more than 15 years ago. *Padre Jesus* had remembered what the ice cream man, *El Profe*, had told him about the concern that many had about Robin losing her gift if she ever found out about the dead friends and relatives in her paintings. *Padre Jesus* felt a little guilty about hiding the truth to Robin, but felt it was best to protect the confidence of his parishioners. After all, he wasn't totally convinced that they were wrong, anyway.

CHAPTER 7

Antonio ran screaming into my office, "They tried to kill *Padre Jesus*! *Dios Mio*! They are insane!"

"What?" I blurted out in disbelief.

"A rancher from Santa Maria just brought him into the Hospital Morazan. They are not sure if he is going to pull through!"

"What happened?" I shot back.

"*Padre Jesus* was making a mountain village visit to Santa Maria with another rancher to bless the rancher's sick cousin when his jeep was blown up by one of those flying bat jets," explained Antonio.

"You mean the military fired on him? Why?"

"I don't know. The rancher riding with *Padre Jesus* was killed and *Padre Jesus* is at the hospital right now."

"Let's get over to the hospital. We'll take my truck. Grab a recorder," I said, reaching for my keys.

The hospital was surrounded by police, military and hundreds of angry parishioners. Still in shock, we waded our way through the crowd, toward the entrance. At first, we were denied access by the marines.

"Look son," I told one marine, "I'm Thomas Clayton from *Radio Onda* and I demand . . ." Just as I started to loose my cool and let him have it, I spotted Colonel Royale in the doorway. Our eyes met at that same moment.

"Let him pass corporal!" shouted Royale. The corporal put down his baton and allowed Antonio and me to pass.

"What the hell is going on?" I angrily asked Royale.

"Calm down Thomas, *Padre* will be alright. Seems we had a little foul up today with one of the military missions near Santa Maria."

"Foul up? Hell, they are shooting at a Priest!"

Colonel Royale was not very convincing as he related to us what he had been told by the U.S. Military about the incident. I found it hard to believe him, and what the U.S. government was saying. I wasn't ready to believe anything until I had a chance to talk to *Padre Jesus* himself.

"Stay here. I will get us permission to go up to where they have *Padre Jesus*," Colonel Royale advised.

As Antonio and I waited, I got more and more upset. Why would the military try to kill a priest and an innocent rancher?

I turned to Antonio, "It's even more important we get to the bottom of this real quick before everything starts to explode on us." I told him that because I know how fear can escalate tension in a city. I was reminded of what Scott and I had stumbled upon back at the temple in the meadows. I wondered if what we had uncovered might in some way be related to what the military was looking for in the surrounding jungles. Were the sounds, the vibrations, the feelings that we were experiencing in the chamber connected to what the military was looking for or what it was listening for?

"Follow me," said Colonel Royale, as he came back to get us.

We walked down the hallway and up one flight of stairs to the room where they were caring for *Padre Jesus*. He looked alert as I approached him. Stepping past a nurse and one doctor, I reached down and put my hand on his right hand. An IV bottle dripped liquids down a tube that was stuck into his left arm. "I'm so sorry. We came just as soon as we heard. Anything I can do for you?"

"I think they are taking good care of me. They tell me that I have a mild concussion and some bruised ribs. I'm still a little foggy as to what actually happened."

"Have they told you the circumstance about what happened to you?" I asked.

"Yes, but I really don't remember much. They tell me I was unconscious for most of the time."

I looked up for a moment, aware of all the people in the room. I looked back at *Padre Jesus* and he knew exactly what I was thinking.

He requested that everyone leave the room because he wanted to spend a few minutes with me alone. As the others left, I pulled up a stool and sat down next to his bed. We both spoke in a softer voice to insure that the others would not be able to hear us.

The pale green stucco walls that surrounded us were muted in darkness; the only light in the room was emitted from a small fluorescent bulb mounted on the wall above the *Padre*'s head. The evening outside had already settled in and turned dark. I noticed a lone picture of Christ holding a lamb hanging on the wall by the window. I felt as if the rolls had been reversed and I was about to receive the confession from the priest.

"Tomas, I am glad you are here. I feel that you are one of the only ones that I can trust. *Don Sanchez* and I had just returned from his cousin's ranch where I gave his nephew a blessing. As we were coming down the hill, another neighbor rancher and his ranch hands waved us down. They had discovered three of the monitoring devices that the military had planted on their land. They wanted to know if we knew what they were. I explained the little that I knew about them and asked if I could have them to take with me into town. I was going to bring them to you. They put them in the back of my jeep and *Don Sanchez* and I bid them farewell. We headed down the mountain through the jungle back to Choluteca. The last thing I remember was a loud boom and a blast of heat. When I came to, I was here in the hospital."

"Thank God you are alive, *Padre*," I said. "The military fired a missile on you. *Don Sanchez* died instantly and you were thrown from your jeep. A passing rancher found you both and brought you here. He told Colonel Royale that one of the jets fired a missile on you as you were driving through the trees."

"But why did they shoot at us? *Don Sanchez* is a family man. He didn't deserve to die this way. It is insanity. I sent Father Domingez to comfort his family."

"The only thing I can guess is that maybe the monitors were still active and with the three all sending out signals from the same location, and a location that was moving toward Choluteca and their base at Camp Semillon in an erratic motion, it had to confuse them.

"They must have thought that the combined signals were something else—a threat to them, even though they couldn't see what it was, or that it was you. They must have fired on you, homing in on the signals from the monitors that were in the back of your jeep." I said as much to *Padre* as to myself.

I told *Padre Jesus* that we were investigating what was going on and I asked him for now not to tell anyone about the monitoring devices that he had in the back of his jeep. I figured that the military should have known what the signals were and shouldn't have been confused. I would later learn that they were hearing several signals. One was the three combined signals coming from *Padre*'s jeep and the other one was actually emanating from deep inside the Temple of *K'in*. The attack occurred less than a quarter mile from the meadows of *Xhutlan*. The addition of that signal, I think, really panicked them. I knew that the military would cover this up as an accident. I looked forward to hearing whatever story is correct in Antonio and Carlos's meeting this weekend. They later would tell us that their communications group thought it had zeroed in on some drug smugglers and had mistaken the padre's jeep for them. Maybe this would slow the military down a little. Whatever they were looking for, the military would have to take a little more precaution because this was an obvious breakdown in procedures and a major embarrassment for both governments.

CHAPTER 8

It was hard to believe that it was already Friday. With everything that had happened around here lately, I wasn't really sure what was real and what wasn't. I needed to get my mind off of everything and just relax my brain, my body and my soul. Getting away with Amaya was just the medicine that I needed. Amaya needed a break, too. I promised myself that I wouldn't think about anything but Amaya and me this weekend. As I pulled up in front of *El Rincon* and parked, I paused for just a moment and looked around me. Everything looked normal. I was a few minutes early. I told Amaya I would be there to pick her up at ten. I wanted to make sure we got out of town before her lunch crowd began to file in because then she would start to worry about leaving. I could hear the doves cooing in the trees across the street in *Parque Central*. The cathedral bells had not gonged out the morning ten bells yet. The shoeshine boys were hanging around a park bench, discussing who knows what. The morning crowd had already gone to work, the lunch crowd was another hour or so off and the park was strangely void of any tourists. Even the *café* in the park was empty. Nothing was moving. It almost looked like one of Robin's paintings. A moment captured in time.

On the other side of the park, out of the corner of my eye, I saw *Padre Jesus* walk out of the Cathedral as another priest opened the heavy wooden doors for him. He was still a little weak from the incident a couple of days ago. He looked a little unstable as he stepped out into the sunlight, looked toward the heavens and stretched a little from side to side. The other priest came up beside him. They both said a few words to each other and the priest went back inside. *Padre Jesus* put his hand up to his forehead to shade his eyes from *K'in's* bright rays and spotted me across the park. He brought his hands together, as if in prayer, and nodded his head toward me as a gesture of hello. I responded with a wave of acknowledgment. Just then, he turned around to look up to the bells to see them chime out the 10 o'clock hour. I stepped down onto the cobblestone street and went in to pick up Amaya.

She was packed and ready to go. We barreled into my truck and left quickly. Once we got off the Pan American Highway, we cut down through the ranches and winding jungle road that would take us to the ocean.

The road, paved about five years ago, looked like it was still under construction. In some areas, it had been washed out by Pacific tropical storms that could turn sleepy jungle streams into fierce raging rapids of frothy dark brown water. The Public Works Department didn't work. They should have called it the Public-Doesn't-Works Department. Some of the washed out areas and even some of the potholes were poorly marked—if they were marked at all. Most of the time a line of washed out boulders that they had taken the time to paint white, was the only warning that you were about to encounter a lack of road. I often wondered if they would be ahead of the game if they spent as much time filling in the washed-out areas as they did painting rocks white. As we came around the next bend in the road, I slowed to watch a flock of scarlet and blue macaws gliding across our path and disappear into the trees. I loved this country. I loved this day. And I loved Amaya.

"*Tomás* let's stop at *La Linda* I need something to drink. Aren't you hungry, *Mi Amor?*" Amaya asked.

"Sure. I'd love some shrimp and a cold beer."

Amaya leaned over toward me and laid her head on my shoulder. "I'm so happy today. How about you?"

"I was just thinking the same."

"The same what?"

"You know," my eyes kept forward on the road as I casually commented, "How beautiful it is here. How much I love this countryside. The jungle. The ranches. The macaws. And of course the potholes!"

"*Tomás!*" she looked up at me and gave me a punch on the arm.

"No, it's true," I said with a grin. "Life is a beautiful journey. God throws in little potholes every now and then just to make sure you are awake."

"*Tomás*, you are so . . . so . . ."

"So, what?"

"You are so good with words, *Tomás*. You make everything sound so beautiful."

"There's one thing that I can't make any more beautiful."

Amaya puzzled for a moment looked out the windshield. Turning her head back to me she inquired, "And what would that be?"

"You . . . You, *Mi Amor*."

Her head was back on my shoulder. Her arms wrapped around my elbow like a pretzel without looking down I could tell she was smiling.

About 20 minutes later I pulled up in front of *La Linda*. Not much of a town. Actually there wasn't even a town there. Just *La Linda*, a combination general store, gas station, post office, restaurant and bar. The other building was across the street. And it wasn't just a building. It was a home. The owners of *La Linda* lived there. Jorge and Elena Castillo and their family opened *La Linda* for all the ranchers and some of the shrimp farmers in the area. It was the midway spot between the Pan American Highway and the town of *Cedeño* on the coast.

Sitting on the front veranda of *La Linda* in her rocking chair was *Mama* Castillo. *Papa* Castillo died a few years ago and *Mama* was the matriarch of the Castillo family. She was a feisty, fun lady. At five foot nothing and tipping the scales at more than 200 pounds, she enjoyed life to the fullest. Believe it or not, at 71, she still enjoyed her evening horseback rides with her grandchildren—after they had finished all their chores, of course. Jorge and Elena ran the day-to-day operations. The older sons took care of the ranch and *Mama* she took care of all her children—young and old alike.

Amaya shared *Mama's* spunk for life. *Mama* always had a special spot for Amaya. I barely got the tires on my truck to come to a complete stop and Amaya was already flying out of her seat, running to the porch.

"*Mama! Mama!*" shouted Amaya.

Every square—or should I say—rounded inch of *Mama* rose to greet Amaya, "*Mi hija! Un beso para mi!*"

"*Ah, Mama!*" exclaimed Amaya, throwing her arms around *Mama.*

I rested my arms over the steering wheel and watched the love unfold in front of me. It was a beautiful day to be alive. Amaya was a free spirit filled with so much love. Her work was consuming her, but it was her passion that set her free. I knew getting away would bring out the Amaya I loved and admired so much . It was a Kodak moment imprinted on my mind. I didn't need a camera. I would be able to remember this moment any time I wanted to.

We caught up on all the news. The lunch was great. The company was the best, and we were back on the road just 20 minutes away from the Plantation House at *Tres Mujeres.*

I rented my *ranchito* from *Señora* Coco, the great granddaughter of the youngest of three sisters who originally owned all the land from the west side of *Parque Central* to the Pacific Ocean.

Three sisters had each married three well-to-do men. One

was a rancher, one a general and one a judge. All three men were killed during a coup in 1829, helping the Honduran armies of Francisco Morazan defeat the northern armies of Manuel Jose Arce, who, at the time, declared himself the President of the *Provincias Unidas del Centro de America*. In 1830 Francisco Morazan was elected to the federal presidency and was considered to be the George Washington of Central America, setting up the independence of the region.

After the death of their husbands, the three sisters gathered their families and pooled their husbands' wealth, buying all the land from downtown Choluteca, west to the Pacific Ocean on the Bahia de Fonseca.

The Three Ladies, or *Tres Mujeres*, as they became known, built a large plantation house along the coast that was run, even up to the early 1930s, as a country retreat for the wealthy of the Honduran capital Tegucigalpa. The tattered, weather-beaten plantation house fell into disrepair for several years before it had its rebirth.

Tres Mujeres is still a small, quiet village where the wealthy continue to go to relax on the sand, dancing away their nights. The original plantation house was finally torn down in the forties and replaced by a 30-room hotel called *La Fonseca*, named, naturally, after the bay that it overlooks.

After we passed the turnoff for *Cedeño*, I headed north along the coast. The ranchlands were behind us. We were in a tropical paradise now. The road cut through the trees that at times seemed so overgrown I felt we were in a tunnel. Dangling vines, moss and palm fronds surrounded us like a tapestry, which was adorned with wild orchards, bromides and cascades of bougainvilleas in reds, purples and oranges. The cries of howler monkeys and parrots created a symphony that seemed to have no conductor. *Tres Mujers* laid about another 12 kilometers ahead of us. To my side of the truck I could see the Gulf of Fonseca through the breaks in the jungle forest. The road finally made its last turn and I saw The Plantation House through the coco palms. I pulled up and turned off the engine. Stretching, I gentling nudged Amaya and she yawned out of her siesta, blinked a little, rubbed her eyes and said, "We are here?"

"Is that a question or a statement?"

"No, *Tomás*. Oh, I don't know—both!"

"I'll get the bellman to get our stuff. Go ahead and meet me at the front desk."

The Plantation House was the center of *La Fonseca* and was the central gathering place for the property, with a front-desk reception area that lead to the Coco Bar and Night Club. The bar was built under a large thatched roof with part of the dance floor under it and the rest under the stars. It had a natural, built-in, first-class view of the setting sun every night. The main building also housed the Cove Dinner Club, a small ballroom and twenty of the thirty rooms. The remaining rooms were individually decorated cabins scattered along the beach.

I had reserved one of the cabins on the point. It had a private beach just a few steps down from the rock outcrop that the cabin rested upon. The bedroom was open on three sides with plantation shutter doors that could all be opened to provide a 180-degree view of the gulf and the vast Pacific.

Across the bay you could see the island of Amapala and three countries all at once. Amapala belonged to Honduras and to the north you could see the coast of El Salvador, and to the south you could see the volcano *Cosigüina*, in Nicaragua. Sir Francis Drake and the rest of the pirates that used to frequent these waters, buried treasures all along these coastal inlets and on the numerous islands that dotted the coastline. I often wondered if it was all still there. If I could only see through the ground and locate it—I would be rich and famous forever. Many have searched for the hidden treasures, yet very little has been found. Occasionally, someone with a metal detector will stumble upon a few old coins but certainly not the hordes that men have dreamed of over the years. I decided it was my time to dream a little and I plopped down on the bed.

"Amaya, honey, I'm going to take a short nap."

"Okay, I'm going to change and go down to the beach and get some sun."

"Can I get you anything before you go?"

"No, *mi amor*, but if you want to bring me something cool down to the beach after you have your siesta, I would love a coco loco . . . *Tomás? Tomás*, did you hear me?" Amaya called out on her way to the bathroom to change.

I did hear her—just as I dropped off to a deep sleep. I don't remember what I dreamed about or even if I was dreaming. I thought for sure I would dream about all that I had experienced during the past few days. True to my desires, I had put those thoughts aside even in my dreams to just enjoy my time alone with Amaya.

"*Señor Clayton. Perdon, Señor Clayton,*" said a voice behind the knocking at the door.

I woke up as quickly as I fell asleep. It was the room service captain with two ice-cold *coco locos*. I thanked him and knew that Amaya must have called down to have the drinks sent to me as my alarm clock. I slipped into to my trunks, picked up the tray and walked down to join Amaya on the beach.

Amaya was soaking in the last few rays of that magnificent Mayan God *K'in*. Looking out over the Pacific, alone with Amaya on our own private beach, I felt like we were the only two people on earth. I absorbed everything around me. I loved the Pacific cumulus clouds like floating white islands in the sky, hanging low, heavy with moisture, like pirate ships laden with gold—their full sails billowing with the wind at their tails. Maybe the spirit of Sir Francis Drake himself was at the helm leading the charge draped out in his finest silks from around the world. I imagined him with his buckles polished, his buttons on his blouse carved from mother of pearl and the golden buttons of his jacket sparkling beneath the rays of *K'in*. He stood in all his regalia, face into the wind and his eyes fixed on the far horizon, his first mate shouting out his commands to all his men. Drake was ridding the high seas again aboard his Golden Hind, in search of more and more treasure to fill his hold. Every cloud telling a different story.

One story the clouds were telling me was that we would have rain tonight. You could smell its freshness as the on-shore breeze mixed in with the salty, musty tropical sea air. I felt like Sir Francis, searching the world for my treasures; my stories. The hull of my ship was full of stories, with room for just one major story left.

I felt my face staring straight into the wind of an oncoming storm of a story that was brewing somewhere back in the jungles and mountains that surrounded Choluteca. My mind began to wander involuntarily. I had to get my mind back to here. I took in a deep breath and closed my eyes. When I opened them, *K'in* was slowly sinking into the Pacific. The clouds were lighting up with rich golden yellows and oranges, with the slightest hint of red. Looking back over my shoulder, I could see the rays striking the coco palms, turning them into Gauguin colors against a deep purple sky above the coastal mountain range. The sand still felt warm under my body, but I noticed a slight drop in the temperature as *K'in* finally sank below the horizon. It was the end of the day, but the beginning of the night. We gathered up our things and strolled back up to our bungalow to shower and get dressed for dinner.

I finished my shower first and told Amaya I would meet her down at the Coco Bar. I could hear the guitar and piano as I walked in and sat at the bar. The hotel was filling up now for the weekend. The bar was crowded with guests and some locals. Most of the clientele was from Tegucigalpa, but it had its fair share of sport fishermen from the United States. Because of the earthquake two years ago off the Baja California coast of Mexico that destroyed so much of the deep-sea fishing business, American fishermen had been searching further for newer areas.

"What can I get you, *señor*?" asked the bartender.

"Dark rum with lime," I replied, still feeling like a pirate. I surveyed the lounge. There were a few couples dancing on the patio, a group of three single women, touristy types sat at the bar sipping on what appeared to be margaritas, and a couple of tables with deep-sea fishermen. Another table had three couples away for the weekend from Tegucigalpa, I'm sure. Two men next to me were speaking French and another man had joined them, speaking German and some broken French. There was one older couple, very elegant. They were deep in conversation with each other while enjoying their bottle of wine. I brought my drink to my lips and the aroma of the rum set the sails in my mind. I was ready for adventure on the high seas.

I quickly finished my first pirates' grog, dark rum and lime. Smooth sailing, I thought, as my second round arrived.

I looked across the room and saw Amaya looking for me. She caught my eye. Her long black hair flowed down her shoulders and swished behind her as she floated into the room. Slightly backlit, her white sarong-like dress was almost transparent. The suppleness of her body was outlined beneath her garment. As Amaya moved, so did the eyes and heads of every man and woman, following her graceful motion. It's the moment that men hate but love. I liked that she was so stunningly beautiful and exotic. It was okay for others to admire such beauty, but it was the erotic smell of testosterone in the room that made me feel uncomfortable, jealous and testy toward the other men in the lounge. I didn't feel the same about the other women ogling her. The "man" thing is, well, just a man's thing, I guess. I've always felt it. I guess because I still have the predator instinct in me. Someday I will grow up and feel secure enough about my own relationships with women. Maybe then the fellings will go away.

Amaya was no dummy. She knew what was going on and she was going to make sure everyone knew she was with her man and only with her man. She walked straight to me. I was still sitting on the barstool. She stood like an ivory statue in front of me. Amaya gently reached up, grabbed my chin, pulling our lips together. She let go, smiled and slid onto the bar stool next to me.

She stretched her arm out and laid her hand on my knee and said, "Your kiss is as sweet as the rum."

"And you, my dear, have just broken many a heart in this bar."

"I know, *Tomás*. But they will mend," Amaya said playfully. "There are plenty of nurses out there."

"What would you like to drink?"

"Actually, I think I will have wine with dinner. I'm hungry after my swim."

"Great, let's go to dinner now." I took Amaya by the arm and we walked out to the Cove. Amaya had lobster on her mind and I was ready for some deep sea bass. Neptune's net awaited us.

Dinner was everything I hoped it would be. We finished up our meals at the same time the couple next to us was finishing theirs. We struck up a conversation with them and learned they were from California. Mike and Maureen had a winter home in Costa Rica and were sailing down from their home in San Diego, California. He and his wife were "retired," so they said. He owned a few businesses back in California, but his son and daughter ran the day-to-day activities. He kept in touch by phone and satellite internet. Their yacht was anchored in the lagoon. They were taking on fuel and supplies and spending two weeks just exploring the gulf while taking up residence at *La Fonseca*. His wife Maureen was a marine biologist. His background was in chemical engineering. The two of them dated through college, married on their graduation night, and after five years of working for two different companies, decided to venture out and start their own businesses. They started a small line of cosmetics, utilizing all natural products found in the ocean. Maureen said her husband Mike came up with their first product, a moisture cream that also had tanning capability without exposure to the sun. They added soaps and a line of fragrances. They came up with a catchy name for the tanning moisture cream: SeaGold. At first it was a big hit with just the beach crowd until they discovered that it had incredible healing abilities for sunburns and even badly injured fire-burned victims. It was marketed to the medical field as SeaCure and the rest is history. Whatever the ingredients were, it was as close to a miracle cure as you could get. There is probably not a house in the United States or a hospital in the country that doesn't have at least one bottle of SeaCure on its shelves. I'm sure that Mike and Maureen were multi-billionaires, but you would never know it. They invited us to join them for a sail the next day over to *Las Islas de Tortuga* to check out the sea turtles. It was the beginning of their nesting season. We gladly accepted and excused ourselves to retire back to our room.

Just as I predicted, the rain started to fall, and we hustled down the path to our cottage. I closed the glass louvers on the south side of the bedroom to keep the wind and rain from coming into the room. We still had our 180-degree view. The storm started off softly and then picked up to a steady tropical downpour. I felt safe and warm inside this old stone cottage. Amaya went off to dress and I waited my turn. The humidity was 110 percent outside in the rain and at least 95 percent inside. It was a comfortable 70 or 72 degrees, maybe a touch cooler with the breeze sneaking through the louvers. Amaya emerged from the dressing room area in a pink cotton terre half-robe.

"It's all yours. I'll turn down the bed," Amaya said as she handed me a big fluffy towel.

"Oh, I get the hint. I'll be right back. Don't go out to play," I teased.

I jumped in the hot shower to wash off the humidity and gradually lowered the temperature to cool me off.

Amaya had turned out the lights and lit candles on the tables and over the headboard. Outside I could still hear the rain coming down. I loved the rain. It always seemed like rain brought good things and happy times with it. "Don't let it rain on my parade" didn't exist in my book. Rain was a blessing from above. I slipped into my favorite flannel boxers and ran the comb quickly through my hair. One last glance in the mirror. Yes, it was me. Look out, Amaya. Here I come.

"Hey, Sweetie, this looks nice," I commented on the lighting as I walked toward the bed. She had fluffed up the pillows and was sitting up against them. The flickering of the candlelight on her silky hair danced about her head. I slid next to her on the bed. She didn't say a word. She just tilted her head a little to one side and looked into my eyes. I returned her look with mine. At that moment nothing else in the world mattered. It was Amaya. It was me. I reached up and touched her cheek with my fingertips and slowly moved them down the nape of her neck and around the back of her head, slowly pulling her face to mine. She closed her eyes and our lips touched. Just a bounce. And then another off her lips. The third had some staying power. Her hands moved around the front of my chest and up to my shoulders and ended around my neck. Our lips were still together. A woman doesn't have to say she loves you. You know from the way she kisses you. There are a lot of different kisses: the friendly kiss, the passionate kiss, the "there you got one now disappear" kiss. But the way a real woman lets you know if she really wants you and really loves you is with the love kiss. It's the unspoken language a woman uses to communicate to her man. Notice I didn't say men. I said to her man. Singular. The love kiss is only given to one, the one that she loves. And if you receive that kiss and can understand the language it is speaking and you feel the same, you just have to communicate back to her in the same language. That's when it happens. There is no mistake. It's as if you share your love and energy together to create more than one plus one makes two. It goes beyond two. It goes on, hopefully, for the rest of your life. When we pulled back to look into each others eyes, Amaya started to speak. I reached up and touched my finger to her lips. She understood. Her lips smiled. Her hands slid down my arm and met my hand. She kissed the end of my index finger and slowly sucked it into her mouth. My finger slid out as she laid her head back to rest it on the pillows. I moved my hand up the side of her body and stretched out next to her.

The palm fronds rattled in the wind against the storm shutters as the rain fell outside and the patio light cast rain shadows which ran down the inside walls of the bedroom.

"*Tomás*, kiss me some more," Amaya whispered.

As we kissed, my hand softly pushed open her pink robe, exposing her piel canela, her cinnamon skin. I continued to kiss her, sliding down the entire length of her curves. Soon we were entangled in passion, perspiration and pleasure. I watched the intensity of her face as it came in and out of focus while we made love to each other.

When we finally both fell back onto the sheets and into each other's arms, we were out of breath and as dripping wet as if we had been out in the rain. It was now a little past two in the morning. The rain had stopped. The palm fronds were still. It was so quiet outside all I could hear were the waves gently lapping on the beach. I looked out over the bay and saw the moon peeking through billowy white clouds. I jumped up, grabbed a towel and threw it to Amaya. "Let's run down for a moonlight swim to cool off!"Amaya hopped off the bed, pulled the towel up to her chest and ran for the patio door. I grabbed myself a towel and ran after her following her tight little butt flying in the open night air.

I woke up first, slipped out of bed and ordered a light breakfast sent to the room. The waiter laid it out nicely on the patio table overlooking the bay: an assortment of fresh-cut fruits, sweet pasteries and rolls, guava juice and coffee. I poured myself a cup of coffee and walked back into the room.

Amaya was still sleeping. I stood for a moment looking at her as I sipped my morning coffee. She looked so beautiful, even when she was asleep. I love that woman. I never thought I would fall in love again, but it happened. I felt so lucky to be alive. She wanted to get married and have a family, and I guess I had been fighting that notion a little ... or, a lot.

I wondered where life was taking me. Something was about to happen—I could feel it. What Scott and I touched upon was way beyond my comprehension, but I think Scott was right. It was time for me to get in touch with my feelings, with the inner side of me. That small inner voice was trying to tell me something: I had to be open enough to hear it. I had to be bold; to follow what I knew inside myself. I couldn't run to anyone else. I needed to run to myself and do what was right for me. What I heard was that I loved Amaya and everything else was of little importance. What was life anyway? I didn't want to be alone anymore. I really wanted love and someone special to share it all with. It was time.

With what appeared to be going on, I knew I might not have much time left to make this kind of decision, but I didn't feel pressured by it. I felt comfortable with the thought of marriage and Amaya being my love, inspiration and partner.

She was already. If I ran from this, I would forever regret it. I kid her a lot, but it was because I loved her so much but was not really totally confident in myself … until now. I realized it I didn't have to wait until everything was perfect, that the journey together is *all about* growth and learning. The trust that you begin a relationship with is the foundation to real love. We had that trust. Now *I* had to trust in us.

Putting down my coffee, I gently sat down on the corner of the bed next to Amaya. I put my hand on her shoulder and softly called her name. "Amaya, Amaya, time to get up."

"Ah, *Tomás*. I want to sleep more," she mumbled rolling over to her side, playing hard to get.

I leaned over, brushed her hair away from her ear and whispered, "Amaya, *Mi Amor*, it's time to wake up. I already have. Not only to the morning, but also to you and me."

This intrigued her. She turned her head back to my eyes and yawned, "Sorry, *Tomás*, what did you just say?"

"I said I am awake this morning more so than I have ever been before in my life. You know, a pretty woman will steal your heart. A beautiful woman will steal your mind. You've done both. Amaya, you are everything I ever hoped for. You are always so loving and outgoing and caring. You tell me in so many ways that you love me. Sometimes you think I don't understand, but I do. What I am trying to tell you, Amaya, is my life could never be complete without you. Amaya, I love you. Will you marry me?"

Tears rolled from her eyes. She stared into mine. "Yes, *Tomás*. Yes. Yes, Yes, Yes!" The yeses came syncopated with kisses and hugs.

Later that morning, we landed on *Las Islas de Tortuga* with Mike and Maureen. They had invited another couple to join us. We had a wonderful time swimming with the sea turtles and watching them struggle up on the beach to build their nests. The mother turtles used their fins to dig out a nest in the sand. It was hard work for them. I could hear them out of breath as they took a rest every so often from their digging. Finally, content with the depth of the nest, they would lay their ping-pong sized eggs upon the sand and then began the hard work of, burying the eggs from predators and providing a secure place for them to incubate. The turtles would then turn around and push and pull themselves back out to sea, leaving the young turtles to grow in their shells. Soon they too would escape back to the ocean.

The crew had prepared lunch for us when we reboarded the "SeaGold." I asked Mike, as Captain of the "SeaGold," if he could marry Amaya and me. He and Maureen loved the idea. We set sail out into international waters for a Pacific sunset wedding at sea.

I called the "SeaGold" a yacht, but it was actually a miniature floating palace. Originally built in 1991, this 195-foot aluminum hull Australian Motor Sailing vessel was powered by twin Diesel Detroit HP2875 engines and carried 31,000 gallons of fuel and 5,800 gallons of water. With its sails and rigging it was also capable of gliding over the ocean solely on wind power.

Amaya was amazed by the galley, which could have put a 5-star hotel to shame. Maureen introduced us to her full time Chef Maurice who delighted in showing us around his galley. It lacked nothing. There were gleaming stainless steel appliances and countertops, a large walk-in stainless steel refrigerator and a walk-in stainless steel freezer with more than 300 cubic feet of space each. Mike took pride in showing us his walk-in, 250-bottle wine vault. What I liked best was the chef's small guest dining table right in his kitchen where guests could have a snack or a full meal plus enjoy the company of the chef as you watched him prepare it right in front of you. Four swivel captain's bar chairs were anchored to the deck, along a high top blue-gray granite table.

The staterooms were spacious and lavishly appointed with two-person Jacuzzi baths. Each of the four guest rooms was decorated with its own theme: Italian, South Seas, Chinese, and my favorite: the Mayan suite. The Oceanic was the master suite. It was as spectacular as it was immense.

Mike told me it measured 30 feet by 36 feet. It was on the main deck, just off the dining room and adjacent main room. The upper deck even had its own barbecue area, pool and outdoor Jacuzzi. Eat your heart out, my pirate friend, Drake. Sailing ain't like it used to be.

We dropped anchor in international waters and everyone, including the crew, was told to join us on the top deck for a special occasion. The sun was just starting to set and the winds had not picked up yet. Captain Mike had the champagne ready and announced to all aboard that they were gathered to celebrate the wedding of Thomas and Amaya. Everyone cheered and gave a round of applause to us brave souls. I looked over and saw that Chef Maurice had even baked a wedding cake on short notice!

Mike stood in front of us and asked Amaya and me to join him. I had to admit it was finally sinking in exactly what I was doing. I took Amaya's hand and we looked into each other's eyes. I really don't remember very much else, but I do remember Mike's final words.

"Thomas Clayton and Amaya Clayton, I now pronounce you husband and wife. You may kiss the bride."

william clyde beadles

CHAPTER 9

Back in Choluteca, it was Saturday night. A time to play and a time to let loose. Saturday nights were party nights here, just like everywhere else in the world. But that night was the beginning of one hell of a night. Carlos and Antonio had invited the marines to a night out on the town, compliments of the radio station. I had told the boys to take them to *El Rincon* for dinner and then out to the *Vaquero* to really kick up their heels.

The young marines showed up right on time—at 1900 hours. They pulled up in front of the *Rincon*, piling out of their Humvee all dressed in their civvies. Marines are experts at camouflage in the jungle. They blend in so well, it is impossible to see them from their surroundings, unless you step right on them. I don't know what it is about taking marines out of the jungle and into a bar; they just don't have the same ability to blend in. Maybe it's their haircuts. Maybe it's the mix of civilian dress that throws them off with too many options. Maybe it's too much freedom to dress themselves. Maybe it's just their attitudes. I don't know, but they stand out like bikers at a church social.

Orlando watched as the *marinos* walked through the front door and were greeted by *Don Pepe*, "*Buenos Noches, muchachos*. Come in. *Don Antonio* and *Carlos* are waiting for you at the bar." Orlando waited until the last *marino* went in, and then he strolled up to the Humvee to get a closer look. He had seen these oversized vehicles rumbling around town but had never gotten up close to look inside one yet. All the electronic gear intrigued him, all the complex instruments and radios, not to mention the weapons that were locked in place around the front panel and on the roof over the back two seats. Those intimidated him. This was definitely a war machine. It didn't come close to the jeeps and Mercedes police vehicles that the local Choluteca Police used for patrols. A couple of other boys gathered around Orlando to check it out, the shoeshine boys from *Parque Central*. Orlando only washed and guarded the vehicles here at *El Rincon*, but he treated every vehicle as if it were his own. He allowed the boys to look for a few minutes, and then he ran them off. After all, this was his turf and he controlled who could be around and who couldn't. They were just shoeshine boys.

K'in shed its last rays on the treetops of *Parque Central*. The streetlights flicked on and the strolling musicians strummed from along the pathway next to the tables at the cantina on the other side of the park. From inside *El Rincon* came the clamor of dinner dishes, laughing and the marimbas from the bar.

Antonio and Carlos stood up to greet the Marines as they walked toward them. They had finished the last of their taping of the interviews this morning. Now it was happy hour. "Hi guys, welcome. You're right on time. See Carlos," said Antonio, turning to Carlos, "you can always count on the marines!" Carlos broke into laughter, as did each marine.

"That's right!" replied Gunnery Sergeant Redman as he extended his hand to Antonio. "Marines are always in the right place at the right time. And this is the right place and this is the right time. What are we drinking around here, anyway? The first round is on me!"

"No. No," jumped in Antonio. "Tonight you are our guests. That means that I pay for everything tonight However, with all due respect to the United States Marine Corp, I will, on behalf of Carlos and myself, accept your kind offer of the first round on you, *Senor!*"

A round of applause broke out among them in response to Antonio's elegant retort. "*Manuel, un trago para todos, lo mejor, y triga la cuenta al Sargento, por favor.*"

"What was that all about?" asked Redman. "Spanish still sounds like a burst of machine gun fire from your mouth."

"That's okay, my friend *Sargento.* Don Antonio just asked of Manuel, the bartender, to come with a drink of his very best for each of us and to make you pay for it." Everyone laughed, along with Carlos.

"Your English is very good, Carlos," said Redman.

"We will have you speaking Spanish tonight before midnight strikes 12 bells on the tower of the old cathedral, I promise," said Antonio.

Everyone was still laughing as Manuel came around the bar with a tray of Choluteca's best. I don't think I even knew what its real name was. Amaya bought it from a family near the coast who had been making *aguardente* for generations. Everyone in *El Rincon* just refers to it as *lo mejor* or the best. Redman took the tray from Manuel and passed out the shots to each of his buddies and then to Antonio and Carlos. Redman raised his glass to make a toast, "Here's to *amigos* in any language!"

"*Sí, Señores! Sí, Señores!*"

"Cheers!"

As they all threw back the first round, Antonio turned to Carlos with a mischievous smile and said in Spanish "*Y que Dios nos perdone para lo que vamos a hacer esta noche.*" (And may God forgive us for what we are about to do this night).

"There you go again, *amigos*," said Redman, turning to Carlos, "Just what did he say now?"

Carlos said with a grin, "He is saying to God that he should bless us all tonight."

"Hey, that's mighty fine with me, too," said Redman.

Antonio turned to Lance Corporal Edmunds and said, "Ready for another shot, Cowboy?"

"Yes sir, if you're a-buyin," said Edmunds, the tallest of the four. Raised on a ranch in Montana, he felt right at home here in the ranching countryside of southwestern Honduras. Decked out in Montana's finest, his boots looked like they had seen a horse or two and his silver belt buckle was one that he had won. Before joining the marines, he won the calf-roping contest in his neighboring state of Idaho at the

Snake River Stampede in Nampa. He was the only one of the bunch that looked like he might have lived in Choluteca.

Don Pepe walked up at that moment and said to Antonio, "*Don Antonio, tu mesa esta lista.*"

"Our table is ready gentlemen. *Por favor*, follow me," said Antonio to the group.

All of the tables in the *Rincon* had been set for the Saturday night crowd. Amaya made sure that every table had fresh-cut flowers for a centerpiece. At the entrance to the *Rincon* stood a huge Chinese vase that she always had amply filled with fresh flowers to greet her customers. Adorned with dragons, a sign of good luck and power, the vase had been passed down through her father's family for many generations, traveling thousands of miles to end up in Central America.

In the inner courtyard, Amaya not only grew her own selection of fresh herbs to use in the kitchen, but also a vast array of fresh flowers. Basil, thyme, sage, lemon grass, mint, oregano, rosemary, mustard, and dill all blended with frangipani, magnolias, lavender, roses, chrysanthemums, poppies, bougainvillea and wild heather all provided a cornucopia of aromas. It gave a sweet earthy texture to the evening air. Here in the tropics she had a built-in, year-round natural garden air freshener. The light evening tropical breeze carried the fragrance throughout the restaurant.

From the back of the restaurant dining area came entirely different aromas, taunting the appetite with well-seasoned meats, fish and fowl, from the large grills where wisps of smoke from the caoba firepits danced above the flames. Diners would watch the chefs cooking over the open flames their individually prepared meals. Major restaurants from New York to L.A. from Paris to Rome would have found it hard to compete with the fine cuisine from this small in-the-middle-of-nowhere restaurant.

"Gentlemen, another round?" Antonio offered.

The Montana kid was ready for more of Choluteca's best. "How about, like you say, another '*lo me whore*,'" jumped in Edmunds.

Everyone laughed with approval at the young cowboy's attempt at Spanish. The waiter knew exactly what to bring.

"I have taken the liberty of ordering for all of us tonight. Carlos and I would like to give you a little taste of *lo mejor en comida* from Honduras. First we will start with *un coctel de camerones del diablo*," said Antonio.

Carlos translated for the men, "*Señor*es, a shrimp cocktail from the devil."

All the *marinos* looked at each other with puzzled looks on their faces.

Antonio quickly explained, "What Carlos means is a delicious giant shrimp cocktail in a special *picante* sauce that we call *Al Diablo* or a devil sauce because of its fine mixture of spices and *jabenero* hot peppers. If the fire is a little too much, in anticipation, I have ordered each of us an ice-cold *Imperial Cervesa* to cool us off a little," smiled Antonio.

"Following the devil will be a cool, refreshing salad of heart of palm and *nopelote* with chilled button mushrooms and seasoned house vinaigrette. Next we will have Choluteca's famous mixed grill: filet mignon *al horno*, roasted garlic sausage, lobster *a la parilla*, red *Huachinango* snapper, stuffed quail and a special local dish that we call *Nacatamales*. Traditionally we serve it around this time and for *La Navidad*, Christmas. We will follow that with a sampling of fine pastries and, of course, the coconut flaming coffee!"

"Coconut flaming coffee?" exclaimed Edmunds. "I gotta see this one."

The waiter returned with the best of Choluteca, and the evening was off to a great start. They all dug into the food when it came, enjoying every last bite. Marines have healthy appetites, no matter where they are.

The highlight was the coffee. It arrived in individual coconuts. Still in the green husks, the tops had been chopped off with a machete; just enough to crack open the top of the brown nutshell. The ivory white coconut meat remained. Inside the milk had been removed and replaced with a special blend of Costa Rican coffee, amaretto, crème de coco, brandy, a little sugarcane syrup and, naturally, Amaya's special secret a touch of *Lo Mejor*. It arrived aflame, burning with a light blue and gold color. Believe it or not, it was as smooth as silk, but it packed a punch. Redman lifted the coconut, and after his first couple of sips, exclaimed, "Here's to the first stealth coffee—silent but deadly!"

Antonio and Carlos had accomplished the first part of their mission. Dinner was over and everyone was ready to party. Antonio settled up with the waiter, and they all went out into the night. The next stop was *El Vaquero*, Choluteca's equivalent of a cowboy dance hall saloon, on the outskirts of town on the road to Nicaragua and the base.

Carlos and Antonio pulled out onto the Pan American Highway and headed south traveling through the banana plantations. The marines in their Humvee followed up the rear. They drove to the outskirts of town and turned off onto a dirt road that leads to *El Vaquero*. The night was just beginning to take shape; the humidity was not too bad as a light breeze kept the sticky sweat from clinging to their skins. The winding, pothole-filled road snaked through the jungle like a large boa, opening into a clearing that looked like the western backlot of a Hollywood movie set. *El Vaquero*, one of four *cantinas* set along a single street carved out of the jungle many years ago, had been a long-time favorite party area for the men and the soon-to-be-men of Choluteca. They could get anything they wanted in this *Zona Rosa*. Even though patrolled by the local *guardia national*, there was basically no law there. It was a free zone where anything goes—even murder, if it was justified, if you know what I mean. Actually, it was quite safe. Everyone has a gun and the last real shootout there was more than five years ago. All the buildings ran down one side of the street; and the other side was for parking and the canal, which fed the irrigation ditches that watered the fields of sugarcane surrounding the small village. In front of the buildings were horses hitched to posts since many of the locals still used working horses for transportation. Others just liked to, well, "ride" into town. Towering mahogany and cypress trees dwarfed the two story saloons.

El Vaquero had the honor of being right in the center of the line of *cantinas*. To one side were the *Nuevo Mundo* cantina, and the *Las Minas* restaurant and general store. To the other side were the *Mujer de Oro* and, at the end of the street, the cantina called the *Tesoro de Los Piratas*, named after the famous pirates that had caused such havoc to Choluteca back in the sailing days.

Both vehicles parked across the street from the *Vaquero*. Everyone followed Antonio's lead. The marines had no fear of this out-of-the-way location totally dominated by the locals. As Antonio's guests, there would be no problems with the locals. Besides they were already slightly intimidated by the soldiers, anyway. They stepped up onto the wooden boardwalk that ran the entire length of the strip and strolled in through the swing doors of the *El Vaquero*. Once inside, the men saw the Honduran version of Hollywood's Wild West. A long bar ran down the entire length of the saloon, with tables in the middle for the patrons and a small dance floor on the other side. There, on a small stage, a local band was knocking out its version of rock *en español*.

"I swear, this place looks like it is straight out of a John Wayne western," commented Edmunds, the Montana Kid.

"Yeah, but look at all the women!" exclaimed Nash. He had hardly said two words all night during dinner. I think the flaming coconuts had finally loosened up his lips.

"Let's take this table over here," said Antonio.

"Looks good to me, boss," said Redman. "Carlos, do they have that *mejor* stuff here? I think I'm acquiring a taste for it."

"No problem, amigo, that is one thing they never run out of here," said Carlos.

"Well, let's see some *señoritas*," shouted Edmunds, as he threw his Stetson upside down on the table.

"Hey, Stevens, look at that gal over there in the green dress. I think this is going to be a night to remember," exclaimed Nash.

"Don't worry, *señor* Nash," Carlos said, "Like *Lo mejor de Choluteca* there are all the young ladies that you can handle. They never seem to run out of them, either."

"*Joven*, bring our friends a round of *Lo mejor por favor*," said Antonio. "Do you like to dance with the girls, *señor* Nash?"

"Yes, sir, I would," replied Nash, now out of his hibernation.

"The night is young and so are the women. Just look around and let me know the one that catches your eye. I let you know what to do from there. Pretty soon you will be dancing up a storm and learning Spanish, all at the same time, I promise," said Antonio. "Just like I promised Redman, before the night bells on *la Iglesia San Antonio* mark 12 you will be speaking Spanish like a native."

Laughter filled the room as the *mesero* put down the first round. "Keep'em comin' *poor faver, senor*," said Redman.

"See Nash, Redman is already breaking into Spanish. It won't be long for you, either," smiled Antonio. "Our interviews will be on the radio next week so all of Honduras will know what our friends find nice about our country."

"Maybe we should have saved a few interviews for what we're going to find out nice about that girl in the green dress," laughed Nash.

"You've got women on the brain, Nash," said Edmunds.

"Yea, well, all you dream about is your damn horse back in Montana," shot back Nash.

"Jealous? I did see a cute little filly saddle horse hitched up out front as we walked in. Maybe I will introduce you later and you can take her for a ride," teased Edmunds. "Nash, you better slow down and switch to beer or you won't be riding anything!"

Nash turned to Walker, who had been pretty much to himself all night. Walker wasn't a very talkative kind of guy. He was the rugged-looking handsome type. He had a deep voice and when he did speak everyone listened because he talked slowly and gently. He wasn't slow. As a matter of fact, he was the most educated of them all. He was one year shy of graduating from college as a veterinarian. He joined the marines just a year ago for some unknown reason. He had been with the Boise Police Department while he was working his way through school. Matt Walker was six-foot- three and every inch of him said "marine."

"Matt, what do ya say we wander over there and pick out a couple of ladies to dance with?" Nash was anxious to get his chance with the *señorita* in the green dress.

"Let's do it! Which one do you want, Nash?"

"That cutie in the green that has been giving me the eye."

"I'll ask the one in red with the long black hair."

"Okay," said Nash, as both men rose and walked across the room toward the band and the table full of women waiting for an invitation. Nash wasn't much to look at, but he had a gift when it came to dealing with women: he was a charmer. And he got what he was after.

Redman watched the men cross the room and looked over to Antonio and Carlos. "I don't know how he does it, Antonio. Nash always gets the pretty ones. I was with Nash in the Middle East and in the Philippines during that last firefight we had with the rebels there. He was never without a girlfriend or two. How about another round?"

"*Muchacho, otra por favor.*"

"*Lo mejor!*" shouted out Redman.

"See, Montana. Redman is already speaking Spanish," laughed Antonio. Everyone was well into the night. With that, Montana got up from the table and left to dance with the others. He headed straight for a cute little gal with long, dark brown braided hair.

Carlos and Antonio sat with Redman, who was starting to get a little sentimental and reminiscent with every shot of "*Lo Mejor*" he kicked back. He'd been around the block a few times. He seemed to have hit the hot spots around the globe the past 10 years. He had experienced a lot and it was beginning to show.

He wasn't a social drinker. He was well past that now. He had become a functional alcoholic. His only escape was the bottle. He had been married three times. No children. He was a lonely man inside where he lived with himself and his drink. It was sad to see what life had done to him. He was probably a very normal, decent kind of guy, but his alcohol addiction had caught up with him and he knew it. He just couldn't accept it. He lived in denial every day. He did his duty and looked forward to his next drink. He enjoyed talking about the good 'ole times. He was a colorful fellow with lots of stories. I'm sure the stories got better and better every time he told them.

He watched the other men dancing, laughing and carrying on with the women when he suddenly turned to Carlos and Antonio and blurted out, "I don't know how they expect us to fight something we can't find and we can't see."

"What do you mean?" asked Antonio.

"I think we are wasting our time here in Honduras. We are supposed to be on a mission to seek and destroy the drug cartel smuggling operation here in Central America. What do we do every day? We plant monitoring devices in the jungle. I don't know what they are looking for. I don't think they even know what they are looking for."

"Redman, who do you mean when you say, *they*?"

"The surveillance teams that they have housed in Hanger 8. They are from the government, I think. They are not military; they don't think like the military. They are after something, something that doesn't exist if you ask me."

"What makes you say that amigo?" Antonio said encouraging him with another shot of Choluteca's Best.

"I took over some reports from the field captain, and I overheard three of them talking about how the intensity of the signal that they have us scouting in the jungle appears to be moving. One said that the strength of the signal is altered by the sunspot activity and that the signal grows in strength every day. I heard one say he thinks the signal is tuning up or something like that. Yeah, the pressure to find the transmitter or the origin of the signal is growing every day around the base."

"Do they have any ideas about what it might be?" asked Carlos.

"Not really. No one has any idea. But I know that they can read the signal from almost anyplace on earth with their satellite systems and from the four space stations. They said that whatever this signal is, it is starting to interfere with other types of communication and navigation systems. I ask one of them while I was waiting to pick up a packet for the Captain, 'Got any ideas as to what or who is out there sending these signals that we are looking for in the jungle?' Know what that asshole said?"

"No, what?"

"He told me, 'Sergeant, it's God.' Can you believe that? They've got us running our asses off on some damn government-funded project, wasting our time and this asshole tells me we are looking for God, as if I was some stupid grunt that had no right to know what they are really looking for."

Antonio shook his head in agreement with the absurdity of the comments, took another sip of his drink and asked, "Why do you have such heavy-duty aircraft at the base if you are just looking for drug trafficker and silly signals in the jungles?"

"Very observant, *mi amigo*, Antonio," said Redman, slurring his speech a little. "I asked that very question to one of the F-1000 pilots last week. Know what he told me? He said, something is out there that is more powerful and *spookier* than you can imagine! I think they are afraid that they might actually find something, and since they don't know what they are really looking for, they are not taking any chances.

It's getting jumpy around the base. This 'spooky' stuff is getting to all of us. I'm afraid that someone might just decide to shoot at something they can't see. And God help us if they actually hit it. They don't even know what they are trying to kill."

"Do you think they would really try?" jumped in Carlos, nervously.

"Who knows? The only spooky people I know are all those government hot shots. They think they know everything when all they know is shit!" said Redman in disgust.

"Well, I think we should call it a night," offered Antonio. Evidently Redman didn't relate the incident with *Padre Jesus*. They were already shooting at things they couldn't see. Better to end the night now before Redman realizes he's shared too much. Carlos went to gather up the troops as Redman and Antonio walked toward the swinging doors.

william clyde beadles

CHAPTER 10

Phones are not supposed to ring in the middle of the night. If they do, it usually is not good news. Coming from a deep sleep in a world and of a state of mind where dreams are real and reality doesn't exist, the rude and intrusive ringing of a telephone is like experiencing an electrocution in your brain. The shock of coming out of a dream into stark reality is a trauma, one we experience every day. It's pain in a millisecond, none-the-less, a trauma. Thank God we forget the transition each time we make it; otherwise we would never wake up. If we remembered everything we dreamed each night, the shock of living each day would be too much to handle. Life has a way of protecting us from trauma. I don't remember being born. I don't know anyone who remembers being born.

I woke up alone and in a state of panic, scrambling to find the phone in the darkness. Hands flying, groping in the blackness, fumbling for a grasp. I'm not sure if I wanted to just stop the ringing or actually find out what the ringing was about.

"Hello," I answered bluntly.

"Thomas, I found it. I found it!"

What the hell was Scott calling me about at this time of the morning? Morning hell! It was still night, only a little past three. He was speaking so fast, so excitedly it was hard to follow. I'm not sure he even knew what he was saying at such supersonic speed.

"The kid in the painting. I met him. He spoke to me. He told me everything. He's . . ."

"Slow down Scott! I'm half asleep," I blurted out. I was just in the greatest lovemaking dream with Amaya and he breaks me out of it. He's my pal, but nothing is worth breaking me out of LaLa Land with Amaya.

"Sorry, Thomas, I just figured it out. *Ciudad Blanca*, Thomas. *Ciudad Blanca*. The kid in the paintings. He's real! He's real! I know who he is. I know this sounds crazy, but I know, Thomas! I *know*! He can take us there!"

"Take us where?" I jumped in, already knowing the answer, but I too got caught up in the excitement. Here, in my dreams, I was just getting it on with Amaya and now I'm talking with Scott about the biggest, I mean the *biggest* story ever told. Now that's pain. How can two ecstasies come at once?

Speaking more slowly now, I finally started to hear what Scott was trying to explain, "Thomas, the kid in the paintings knows where *Ciudad Blanca* is . . . he, I think, lives there. Robin has unknowingly painted him into the backgrounds of five of her paintings. Five times. The same kid. He's in her latest one that she just finished tonight of Lori on the soccer field at school. Thomas, this kid is not a kid. I don't know how to explain it. But this kid is not a kid. He knows too much. It's scary. I don't know how to explain it. I only know what I feel. What I sense. Thomas, you have to come with me. Meet me tomorrow at the *Rincon* at five."

"Scott, this is already tomorrow!" I said, "It's three-thirty!"

"Oh, yeah," replied Scott sheepishly.

"Scott, this is crazy. What you are saying is 'come now!'"

I took a quick shower and drove into town. It didn't take very long at this ungodly hour of the morning. I don't know what was flying faster—my mind or my suburban. Scott was really excited. I don't think I have ever seen him this out of control. *El Rincon* opens at 5 a.m. every morning. The ranching community gets an early start to each day. I only had a few hours of sleep. It seems like I just dropped Amaya off from our weekend a few hours ago. There to greet me was *Don Pepe*. I thought to myself: "This man will never die in his sleep. He never sleeps."

He is also never without some social commentary. *Don Pepe*, as I passed by, said *"Buenos días, Tomás.* I see you are having trouble staying away from this place. Maybe you might like to become Amaya's partner in *El Rincon* business?"

I turned my head and gave him a quick smile. He gestured with both hands, palms turned up, tilting his head back a little and slowly rolling his eyes up to the ceiling, as if saying "why not?"

I slid into my regular table on the patio. At this early hour, I had it all to myself. My first cup of hot coffee hit the table about the same time I sat down.

"*Algo más, Don Tomás*?" said the bus boy. I even beat the waiter here. He must be running late. I told the bus boy I didn't need anything else until *Señor* Hoggan arrived. I sipped my coffee and looked up at the old German wall clock. It was five minutes past five.

The city was just starting to wake up as an occasional person wandered down the cobblestone Avenida Vasquez in front of the patio. I looked over my shoulder in the arch of the walkway and saw Amaya's smiling face peeking around the corner.

"*Otro café, señor* Handsome?" She said acting as if she was some waitress coming onto me.

"Only if you come a little closer, I could tell you exactly what I want," I played along.

From around the archway she stepped out onto the patio and walked to me with the steaming pot of coffee held out with one arm, "Sorry Mister, only *café*."

"Okay, as long as you share a cup with me," I replied.

Amaya sat down and filled my cup and poured herself one. "What are you doing here so early? You should have just stayed here. You know that I could have arranged it," she smiled.

"Don't worry; I think your *Don Pepe* is already working on it. Anyway, Scott called in the middle of the night and told me he needed to see me here first thing this morning. So here I am and there he is now," I said.

I looked up to the clock on the wall. It was 15 minutes past five. Scott was late. He jumped out of his Land Rover.

He knew he was late and was trying to make up for it with every stride he took. He turned quickly at the corner and entered the *Rincon*, never breaking his stride. Amaya got up to greet him and then walked back to the kitchen. Sliding into his chair, he tossed his hat and took off talking, just where we left off on the phone a short while ago. Ever since I have known him he was never without a hat.

"I know who the kid is! Remember the night that you saw some kid go into the jungle and Bark was acting strange? Well, even though I didn't see him then, I have before but didn't know it. I started looking in the background of some of the people in Robin's paintings, and there he is. He's not in every painting, but I have found him in five of them. The most recent is the one Robin just finished last night. She took some pictures of Lori at her school, playing with her classmates on the playground. In the background, outside the fence looking in, is this kid in her painting. But he wasn't in the original photograph she took for some reason, but she still painted him in. I asked her if she had seen this little boy before, and she said no. She photographs her main subject and just fills in other people to add interest where needed. She is totally unaware that she has included this kid in four other paintings. I didn't tell her that I had noticed him in the other paintings. I'm not sure what we are dealing with here yet. Before going home last night from *Xhutlan*, I had this feeling that someone was watching me. You know, you've experienced that feeling before, I'm sure. Standing near the tree line in the meadow was this kid, just watching me. It was as if he wanted me to see him. I stopped what I was doing and we just stared at each other for a few minutes. I finally called to him and motioned for him to come near. He walked slowly but confidently toward me. I wasn't really sure what I should do, so I just put out my hand and said hello. He took my hand with both of his and simply smiled," said Scott as he took a pause to drink some coffee.

"What did he say?" I asked.

"I said to him again, hello, my name is Scott Hoggan. He said yes, I know. My name is *Utmal* and I live in the jungle," Scott said.

"How did he already know your name?" I was curious.

"Thomas, *Utmal* knows everything. He told me he knew about my daughter and that she was going to die. He said that he lived in the jungle in a place no one could see. A place where there is no pain. No sorrow. No disease. I was mesmerized. He spoke to me as a child but with manly words and expressions. I guess his age to be about the same as Lori's. I felt a strong calmness come over me as he talked. He told me to meet him here tomorrow. He also told me to bring my daughter Lori, and he would take us to his city and change my life and the life of Lori's forever," Scott said.

"You think it could be some kind of a trick or ambush or something?" I questioned.

"No, Thomas I don't. I really can't explain it. There seems to be a lot going on that I can't explain right now, but I have a feeling. Remember what I have said before. Whatever is going on around here goes way beyond normal linear thinking. It's feelings that seem to be talking to me. I don't really mean talking to me, but innately guiding me toward what I am looking for. It's not just wishful thinking or faith. It has an action element to it. I know that there is no city out there. But he says there is one, but no one can see it. It reminds me of *Ciudad Blanca*. I feel that this just might be *Ciudad Blanca*. I feel like we are on the edge—on the edge of something very big. I sense it, Thomas. I need your help again. This could be a very emotional encounter for me with my daughter. I want you to come with us. How about it, my twin brother?" Scott asked anxiously.

"My answer to your invitation goes without saying! Of course I'll be there. What time are we supposed to meet him?" I asked.

"I told him we would be there around four in the afternoon and I would have Lori with me. I told Robin I would be in town for a meeting, and I had promised Lori I would take her out to the site for a little while after she gets out of school. She said that was fine. I'll pick you up a little after 3:30 here at the *Rincon*, and I will drop the other kids off for her at her shop," Scott said.

"I'll just follow you out in my truck, so you won't have to bring me back into town," I told Scott.

I was starving, so we ordered breakfast. When we finished, I said goodbye to Amaya and drove straight to the station to see what the guys had found out with their night out with the marines on Saturday.

Antonio and Carlos were waiting for me outside the station as I pulled up. They couldn't wait to tell me what they had found out.

"Let's go inside and talk," I told them.

They started to fill me in on what was going on right when we felt another earthquake. This one was very strong. "Get everyone outside *now*!" I screamed.

No sooner were we out the door when another one hit. This one felt stronger than the first. Some windows in the station started to pop, glass crashing to the ground. The transmitter towers swayed a bit, but they were built to take the shock, whether from an earthquake or a tropical windstorm.

"Is everyone okay?" I called out. "I want only the on-air staff to go back inside. The rest stay outside for now. Antonio, check to see where the epicenter was and what we have on the wire. Carlos, do a walk through the building to see if we suffered any other damage. Have Roberto be ready to go on emergency power and then check the transmitter and the towers."

I called Amaya from my cell phone. She was okay. They had some damage in the bar and some dishes in the kitchen fell over but nothing too serious.

"Boss," Antonio said. "We felt about a 5.2 here but the epic-center was located just offshore from Okinawa in the western Pacific. The preliminary is above a nine. They said it generated a tsunami, causing massive damage to the southeast coast of Japan, the coast of mainland China, Taiwan and the Northern Philippines. They are estimating casualties in the hundred thousands. It hit there right in the middle of the night. It must have been utter chaos. Those poor souls," Antonio said, lowering his head in respect for them.

"Get it on the air and cut the regular programming until things settle down. Have Carlos get on the phone and call around to see what damages we have locally."

"*Jefe*, we have one tower signal knocked off so we're not getting full coverage. I can have it fixed in about two hours. I will have to go to half power for about 30 minutes to an hour while I replace some parts," informed Roberto.

"Do your best!"

"*Sí, Señor.*"

"Carla, can you stay and take care of the switchboard?" I asked.

"Yes, *Tomás*, I will be fine."

"Okay, Carla, send the rest of the staff home to see if everything is all right with their families."

I went back into the newsroom to see Antonio and Carlos. Antonio was on the air and Carlos was manning the wire services and the satellite. Carlos put down the phone and handed me a Teletype. "*Tomás*, look at this. The whole Pacific Rim is feeling this. Colorado is saying that it may be closer to a nine than an eight. Hawaii is reporting volcanic activity on the Big Island and two other volcanoes in the Pacific have gone off—one in the Philippines and the other in the Aleutian chain in Alaska. Nicaragua reports that Monotombo is spewing smoke and gas."

"Take this into the studios and you put it on the air. Send Antonio in here to see me."

Antonio walked in from the on-air studio and grabbed a cup of coffee. "Looks like we got off lucky here."

"So far so good, it seems. How did your night out go? Learn anything new?" I asked.

"You were right about the listening devices. They are

planting them everywhere, trying to figure out where some weird, unusual signals are coming from. They said that the signals move around, so they haven't been able to identify them. They also said that they are growing in intensity to the point that they are starting to interfere with other radio and navigational signals. They say that they are picking up the signals all over the world, but they seem to be emanating from somewhere around here. Redman said that the *narco traficantes* story is just a cover up and that the base has a secret non-military group in hanger eight. They are the ones that are controlling the clandestine operation."

"What about the F-1000s? What are they all about?"

"Yeah, I asked him about them, too. He said that he had talked to some of the pilots. Here's what he said about them," Antonio went on, "The pilots say they are searching for something that they can't see, but they know something is out there. He says they are 'spooked and on edge'. Because they don't know if it is some kind of terrorist threat or some kind of worldwide jamming device, they are taking no chances. Everyday it seems to grow more intense. Oh, yeah, he also said that the sun has something to do with it, too, something about sunspot activity causing the signals to intensify. They are ready to start blasting pretty soon—at what I don't know, and Redman thinks the same. They are under a lot of pressure to find the location where the signals are being sent out. That's about it, boss."

"So no one has any idea what or who is causing all this interference? Not even some wild guesses?" I was reaching for anything. Anything.

Antonio thought for a second and then said, "Well, Redman did say one sort of crazy thing. He doesn't like the government workers calling the shots with the military. He thinks they are talking down to him. He told me he had asked one guy if they had any idea who was sending out the signals."

"Well, what did he say?" I inquired with curiosity.

Antonio laughed a little and said, "He said the government worker looked at him like he was some kind of hick and sarcastically told him . . . *God.*"

"God?"

"Yes, God. That's what he told him. And Redman was really pissed at him for trying to make him look like a buffoon."

william clyde beadles

CHAPTER 11

The jungle is a wild and primitive place. Even today the word jungle conjures up mystery and intrigue. As we walked with Scott's daughter, Lori, to the site, I was a little wary of what to expect. My nine-millimeter tucked in my pants under my *guayabera* shirt gave me a sense of security. Scott understands hope and mystery more than I do. I'm a skeptic, yet inquisitive. It's my nature as a journalist.

As we rounded the bend in the trail, we entered the meadow of *Xhutlan*. Sure enough—sitting on the edge of the clearing across the meadow was *Utmal*.

He smiled and stood up as we approached. Scott greeted him, "*Utmal*, we are happy to see you."

"Happy to see you come here," *Utmal* said, staring somewhat shyly at Lori.

This was the first time I saw the little boy in him.

"*Utmal*, I want to introduce you to my daughter, Lori," Scott said, as he gently laid his right hand on her shoulder.

"Thank you very much," he said and, with a soft bow of

his head, he turned to *Tomás*.

"And this is my friend Thomas. I asked him to come today to help us," Scott said.

Looking into my eyes, *Utmal* politely said, "I understand." He quickly turned back to Scott and said, "We walk."

Utmal turned into the jungle and we followed. He looked back every few minutes. It seemed he only wanted to make sure that Lori was still with us. Or maybe with him. We crossed a shallow stream and came to a large rock. It sat alone on a small sandy island. *Utmal* pointed to it and said, "This is *Walpa Ulban Tara*." The large boulder blocked the natural flow of the stream. The water surrounded the boulder, passing to each side from upstream and reforming on the side we were approaching to form a tiny island. *Utmal* stopped and said, "We are here."

The large rock looked slightly familiar. Then it hit me. I turned to tell Scott, but he was way ahead of me.

"Thomas, it's a duplicate of the boulder platform in the chamber!" Scott whispered.

It looked the same to me, but it didn't have the steps and handholds carved in it. It looked like just another large boulder, fitting in perfectly with the rocks around it.

Scott and I looked puzzled, but Lori said, "Let's go in."

What did she mean? What was she thinking? *Utmal* turned sideways and motioned with his hand, arm extended to enter. His arm was halfway in the rock and halfway out.

The hair on the back of my neck stood up and a chill shot through my body. This is not real. It's a dream. But I'm not dreaming. It's not . . . it can't be. I looked to Scott. He had a bewildered look on his face, too. Yet I could see that he somehow knew it would be okay.

Lori, with a childlike fascination and faith, only wanted to follow *Utmal* into the rock to experience the fun of the adventure she imagined in her mind. To her, it was just a game. Something fun.

Scott took Lori's hand and they walked into the rock. At that moment, three dimensions, as I understood them simply disappeared. *Utmal* looked at my bewilderment and simply said, "*Tomás*, you will not have need of that," and smiled as he pointed to the bulge under my shirt.

I believed him, and slowly and almost embarrassed, pulled my 9-millimeter Smith and Wesson from my waist and set it down on the ground. Three steps later, I was in the rock. As we looked around these new surroundings, it appeared the same. It just felt different. I felt safe for the first time in my life. Completely safe.

We walked only a few steps more when we arrived at the edge of the lost city Scott had dreamed of finding. *Ciudad Blanca*! Scott was right. It was real. Or was it? What did we really just experience? We weren't drugged, hypnotized or anything else. Were we really even here?

Utmal led us down a street toward the city center. People watched politely as we stared in excitement and reverence at the same time. Life looked normal—the same. It seemed we had just walked through a shield or a gateway or that a vortex had consumed us. As we walked, I could feel sound and light, shadows, colors and time. Not just see or hear, but feel. I could actually feel color and light. I could close my eyes and feel red, blue and green. I could feel the difference between light and dark. My body seemed to be like a filter that allowed everything to freely enter it, flow through it and exit. Every color and every shade of color also had its own sound. Not only could I feel color, but I could also distinguish each color by its own unique sound. Light. Sound. Color. Touch. Everything was alive. The city was vibrant. The Mayan ruins that I had seen all over Mexico and Central America were mostly a stone gray or tan color. The years and the elements had washed away all the color that was originally covering them. These buildings and temples looked like they were brand new, as if they had just been painted minutes before we arrived.

"Welcome to *Xhutlan*. This is my city. It is the city that you like to call *Ciudad Blanca*," said *Utmal*, turning to Scott. "We have been living here in this valley for thousands of your years. Here we have peace. Here we practice patience and eternal life. We have a mission, but you will learn more about that later. Follow me," *Utmal* said.

As we walked toward the city center the inhabitants or, I should say the ancient Mayans, smiled and gave a gentle drop of the head. I assume it was their form of greeting and acceptance to our presence. I returned the gesture, rather awkwardly, I might say. I have to admit I was still feeling out of place, but in a humble sort of way. The Mayans had a certain radiance and grace about them. Not the fierce warrior images that somehow I had associated with them from history. The sacrifices, blood-letting, battle-dressed warriors and powerful—even vengeful-like Mayan Gods all seemed out of place here. My hardness or edge was softening. My skeptical nature was fading and I felt myself becoming more accepting, more open to not judging. Maybe this is what I have heard some people refer to as a "change of heart." Scott had asked me to be the documentarian. The eyes. The ears. The reporter. He was very emotional about this meeting and wanted to go with his feelings. It was as if some small voice from deep inside Scott had spoken to him. The voice was telling him to trust his feelings and let him be guided by them. I have to admit I was hard pressed to keep my professional, journalistic approach up. I felt that calmness that beckoned me to surrender to its persuasions. The tension that initially had a grip on my body, mind and judgment was quickly dissolving as I surrendered more and more with each step. It was not surrendering in the sense of giving up. It was surrendering a negative to find a positive, calm, reassuring replacement. I felt the more I let go the more I gained. All my senses were coming alive. They were keener. Sharper. More acute. I felt the warmth and the brilliance of the light of the sun, but I could not see it in the sky. It was a strange sensation.

"Scott, look up. Where is the sun?" I said softly to him.

"You're right."

"There are a few scattered clouds, but no sun. Where is the light coming from?"

"I don't know, Thomas. I can feel it, but I can't see it."

"*K'in* is everywhere. Everywhere you are. You just don't know where you are yet," said *Utmal*, overhearing our conversation.

He was right I thought. Not only don't I know where we are, I really don't know *why* we are here. I'm not even sure if "here" is "here."

We arrived at what appeared to be the city center. In front of us was an extremely large pyramid dwarfing everything in sight. Its base was close to being the length of two football fields. The height was about 10 or 12 stories. It was flat on top, not pointed like the pyramids of Egypt, and was made of a gray-white stone. Looking up the face of the pyramid at certain intervals, there were brightly colored murals that ran horizontally across the face. These brightly painted murals ran like bands around the entire pyramid. Each one had a different theme to it. The center of the pyramid had two flights of block stone stairs. They were separated by colorful carved-stone images that were in contrast to the natural stone of the steps. Each carved stone image was elaborately painted. Each represented different Mayan rulers and deities. The inhabitants of this town were moving up one side of the stone stairs to the top and down on the other side to the bottom. The only problem was they were not climbing up or down the steps. They seemed to float up and down each side almost as if being on an escalator but the stone steps weren't moving—just the people were. Lori didn't seem to notice, but Scott did.

He slowly asked me, "Are you seeing what I *think* I am seeing?"

"Looks like we are going to go for a ride." I looked to *Utmal* and, in his own way, he gestured to us to take the first step on our own. We all stepped together onto the first stone step and sure enough, we were floating slowly toward the top. *Utmal* was two steps behind us, simply smiling.

The only way I could describe the ride was that it was just like riding on an escalator, but the escalator wasn't moving— we were. People always have a problem getting on and off an escalator because it is moving. There was no sense of that feeling or a sense of loss of balance. It actually was quite neat. I turned my head around to look out over the city as we rose. It was an awesome sight.

Ciudad Blanca stretched out across a lush green valley that was surrounded by gentle rolling hills. A meandering river wound its way through the city and disappeared into a canyon at the base of the hills. On either side of the river were agricultural areas and terraced hillsides. The jungle canopy divided areas of developed farmlands. The jungle gradually turned into forests as it climbed up the hillsides. I could see Mayan farmers working their fields and cattle grazing in velvet-green pastures.

Directly below, I could see the myriad of people going about their daily chores around the city. Everyone looked busy and content. I did not notice a single person that appeared to be poor, rundown or unhealthy in any way. I saw many artisans and craft makers when we first approached the base of the pyramid. They were going to and from the central market area, or trading area, much like the open-air markets in Choluteca. As we floated higher, they became like scurrying ants.

Reaching the top of the pyramid, I found it to be a flat stone surface with two small buildings at either end. In the center was an arena that held about four or five hundred people seated around what I would call a Shakespearean stage or theater in the round. As we approached the entrance to the arena, I noticed something else that was not present. Nor were they present at any point along the route from the rock to here—guards or warrior types. There seemed to be a complete absence of security. That feeling of calmness and safeness that I was sensing was so strong. I wondered if the others and those living here felt the same. Maybe that is why I did not see the presence of guards or any army or security force. Scott did say earlier that *Utmal* had told him his city was one of peace.

We followed *Utmal* to the center of the platform, atop the pyramid where the stage was located. Standing in the center of the stage were three men and two women. They had been addressing a crowd below, but stopped as *Utmal* and all of us entered the arena. Their dress was as colorful as the city. They still dressed in the ancient Mayan ways, with beautiful cloth garments adorned with feathers, shells, silver, gold, copper and gems of many colors. The one I assumed to be the leader of the group was dressed mostly in different shades of purple, with yellow feathers. His garment was embroidered with gold and silver thread. His long, dark, black hair hung straight to his shoulders. His dark eyes and chiseled face were rich in strength yet possessed gentleness at the same time. No one seemed alarmed at our presence or dress. *Utmal* stopped short of the stage and, with a slight bow of the head, he said, "Father, I have come from there. I have brought you the little girl I spoke of, and this is her father and his good friend."

Utmal turned to us with his arm extended and motioned for us to come forward. We stepped up onto the stage with *Utmal* and greeted the group.

Out of the group before us, one man stepped forward. He was the one I assumed to be the leader. "I am *Mytar*, the father of *Utmal* and the first King of my people. We have lived here since the beginning of our time. We call the place where we live *Xhutlan*. My people and I have been chosen to live here until the end of our time, which you already know is drawing close. We are the guardians or gatekeepers to the next world or time. We hold certain powers and promises that will be given to those of the next generation of time. We have lived with these powers for thousands of your years, learning their meaning and significance. My people and I are ready for this new world that is coming. We will be the instructors to the new world, as you will come to know it. We are here to help you and all the other inhabitants of your world to make the transition into the new time. *Utmal* has told me many things about your lives. I feel as if I already know you, Scott and *Tomás*. If you would allow me, please have Lori step forward to me."

Without any hesitation, Lori freely stepped forward into the arms of *Mytar*. He gently embraced her and whispered something in her ear. She smiled and turned around to face us. *Mytar* was standing behind her. He held his hands to his sides and he literally walked through Lori's body and out the other side. He was now in front of us, with little Lori behind him. He smiled to us and turned around to Lori. This time she embraced him. *Mytar* took her hand and led her over to Scott and said, "Have no more fear for your daughter's well being." He nodded his head in a gesture of peace. He then told *Utmal* to take Lori and show her around while he talked to us.

Mytar asked us to sit with him and the others. I was no longer afraid of anything he was about to tell us. Calmness came over me and all the confusion I had been feeling was gone. This inner peace consumed me and I became like a dry sponge, waiting for my chance to soak in everything. Scott didn't have to say a word. I could read his face as if he were talking directly to me. His spiritual feelings were much more developed than mine.

"You men have entered into a world that is both under and above life and also everywhere in between. You are going to learn many things, and you will understand every word of what I will tell you. I was given this gift. I am passing it onto you Scott, and to you, *Tomás*. Your world, from which I began too, and the one that I live in now, are about to collide. Your world is coming to its end. Do not be saddened because as you will soon learn, the new world is about to begin. With it there will be riches and opportunities that men have only dreamed of throughout their lives on this earth. There have been many great men and women throughout the ages that have contributed significantly to this life of yours. There are also those who have followed a different path. One of greed, pride and destruction. They have suffered already and their future estates will be one of service, with a chance to learn a new way of living. For now, they will not find the opportunities that you will have the chance to encounter. You both have been silently and internally harboring personal goals in your lives. Scott, you have found your *"Ciudad Blanca,"* and *Tomás,* you will have your greatest story ever told. However, in this life, you will not be able to tell anyone of these accomplishments. Your rewards will await you in your next life. They were honorable goals, but your goal now is to protect this knowledge from the world for a few more days. No one is to know of your mission. You are both just and fair men who have been chosen to take care of this task," said *Mytar.*

I looked to Scott and he returned the glance. We were ready to find out exactly what would be required of us.

Mytar continued, "In the new world, you will experience 12 dimensions and receive one promise and one warning. You are well aware of the first three dimensions and you have quite a good idea as to what the fourth dimension is because you are experiencing some of it right now. It is the ability to see and move within the first three dimensions. You saw me walk through your daughter, Scott. I could see the cancer in her blood tissues. All I did was filter them out with my body and then let them pass from me. Your daughter is completely cured. The leukemia will not return. With this dimension you will learn to eliminate all disease, all surgeries, and be able to cure any ailments, simply by rearranging the matter before you. You will learn that the riches of this world are not the ones of the new world. With the fourth dimension, you will be able to look into the ground and see as far as you want to see. You can see a diamond or a gold nugget three inches down or 100 feet down. With the fifth dimension, you will learn how to travel through the fourth dimension," *Mytar* explained.

He went on to say, "The fifth dimension allows us to travel without the passage of time. You can literally be in two places at once. You will be able to move in and out of objects freely. You will be able to move back and forth in time. Not time travel, as you know it, but the ability to travel to where you want to be in the same time. You can evaluate where you want to be and not lose time in your exploration."

Mytar continued, "It will be as if time is put on hold until you decide where you want to be. Speed does not exist in the fifth dimension. Speed relative to time, that is. You will be able to move anywhere on this earth and not have to worry about the loss of time in travel. You are standing here before me right now and, if you want, we can be standing on the other side of the world at the same time. You can't be in both places, but you can be in either place. At any given point in time you can be wherever you want to be and not take time getting there. Being does not involve motion. You are constant. You are you wherever you are. Time is simply a measurement of movement. Without motion, there is no movement in time."

"The sixth dimension," he added, "will give you the power and ability to control our minds and emotions. You will learn how to focus your thoughts and have full use of your brain. You will never forget anything you do, see, hear or feel. You will be able to call up this stored knowledge at any time. If you are verbally or emotionally attacked, you will be able to center yourself and find your way through any situation. You will no longer fear aggressive or combative situations. Your mind will be clear; your emotions stable. Worry will not exist. Your own emotions will be enhanced and have more dimensions to them. Your life will be richer and your experiences fuller. You will learn what it is like to have peace on earth and tranquility with your soul."

"Along with the first six dimensions comes a promise. The promise is that once you have mastered the entire first six dimensions, no one or force or thing will be able to deny you of these first six. The promises of these first six gifts are with you forever . . . for all eternity. You will learn more about how to use these dimensions and six more upon your return. After you have learned to master all 12 dimensions, you will be given a warning . . . ."

There was a pause as *Mytar* looked us both in the eyes. He asked us to stand and come near. He extended his hands and placed one on my head ever so gently and the other on Scott's.

"We are all brothers in spirit, each of an earthly family. We are about to embark on a new and glorious mission to a new beginning. I pass on to you the gift of knowledge of things that are to come, those that have been and those that are. Even those things which eyes have not seen, ears have not heard, or felt those things yet to be entered into the hearts of men. Listen to what is inside you and you will find that even the mysteries from the days of old and for the ages to come will be revealed to you. You will know the wonders of eternity and with this power and inner spirit, you will be enlightened. Go and prepare for the end and the beginning. Listen to all that is you. Listen to your inner self and to the power that enters you to fulfill that which you have been asked to fulfill."

With that, he put his hands back to his side and, looking us both in the eyes, he told us, "Return to us here in three days and you will receive the fullness of what is to come. Now go with the power of knowing that you can prevail to the end. Listen, and you will be guided by the spirit from within you."

Never in my life had I felt so empowered and so confidant. As his hands lifted off my head, I looked up to his face and I saw eternity staring back. I was on the edge of the beginning.

CHAPTER 12

I had a hard time sleeping through the night. Yesterday's trip to *Ciudad Blanca* was something out of a science fiction story, but it wasn't science and it wasn't fiction. Maybe, like my dreams, it was only fact based on fiction. Fact based on fiction. Had the tables of reality turned on me? Not just me, but all of mankind. Was it history? Was it theology? Was it myth? Was it science fiction? Whatever it was, it was real in my mind. I think.

"*Tomás, levante, Tomás*," Called out Tida.

"I'm already up," I shouted back, even though I wasn't yet. "Just coffee and *jugo* please." I laid in bed stretching out the muscle kinks in my back. Amaya and I were keeping our marriage a secret for now. We planned to settle in here after the holidays and just keep our small quarters at the restaurant for those times when we really didn't want to come out here to *Los Ranchitos*. Amaya had a couple of very good managers that she trusted. It would be easier for her to pull back a little, so we could spend more time together. Just like me. My radio station pretty much ran itself. All my crew really worked together as a team. They were a family unto themselves. Everyone looked after each other.

I slugged down my coffee and fresh-squeezed orange juice picked this morning from my own orange trees and headed into the station. I needed to talk to Roberto about trying to build a series of decoy transmitters to throw off the military and buy us some time if we needed it. I had this crazy idea during the night. I kept thinking about what *Mytar* had told us about protecting the knowledge we had received. *Mytar* seemed to be concerned the military would interfere in some way, so Scott and I had been appointed to be the Hero Twins sent to defend time. The only thing that tugged at me was what did *Mytar* mean when he said, "With all of this would come a warning." A warning? Out of all this positive karma, he ended with what I took to believe was a negative thought. A warning. A warning of what? A warning to whom?

As I approached Choluteca, I noticed three helicopters flying in formation to the north of town. They were flying a grid pattern as if they were mapping the area. It was actually a grid search they were flying, obviously still trying to find that signal.

I arrived at the station just as Roberto was pulling up. "Roberto, good morning. Everything all right?"

"Yes, except for those damn helicopters."

"Why, what's going on?"

"Last night they started night flights over my farm and the surrounding area. They flew all night long, back and forth. Back and forth. The kids got up once but went back to bed. Ana and I were up the rest of the night."

"They are still going at it just north of town. I saw them as I was driving in this morning."

"Do you think they are going to keep it up?"

"I'm afraid so, Roberto. I need to talk to Antonio for a few minutes, and then I want to spend some time with you. I've been doing a little thinking, and I have an idea that I would like you to help me with . . . sound okay?"

"Sure, *Jefe*, I'll be back in my shop when you need me."

I walked back to the studios and found Antonio and Carlos working on their upcoming news reports.

"What's the latest?" I inquired of the two.

"*Hola, Tomás*. The world is going crazy or something. We've got stories from all over the globe. I've never seen so much news all at once in my career," Antonio answered. "Dramatic weather all over the place; civil unrest in Europe; the Pacific Rim is living up to its reputation as the ring of fire; some kind of strange disturbance with navigation systems, causing flight delays everywhere. The military has gone on full alert: Force Protect-Condition Delta. They are blaming it all on sunspot activity, and it's causing a lot of problems with international security. Evidently, they are witnessing some of the worst solar storms ever recorded. The fires in Australia are the worst on record there. They have burned all the way to the ocean and about a third of Adelaide is on fire on the west side. The World Health Organization just announced that the fight against cholera is over. No new reported cases in the last 24 months. They are saying that it no longer exists. On the other hand, the Center for Disease

Control in Atlanta is reporting the new AIDS virus, HIV-4 now has infected 24 million people worldwide and the death toll for the first three quarters of this year is at two million and rising."

"Seems our little problems here are dwarfed by what is happening elsewhere," I commented sadly.

"We are receiving fewer complaints about the military here and more calls about concerns in other parts of the world."

"That's good for us right now with the locals, but the military is still up to something. I am concerned that they are getting more and more desperate with each day. I've got an idea on how we can flush them out, Antonio," I told him, not wanting to let him know exactly what I had up my sleeve. My plan was to set up decoys to confuse the military if I need to, and I was quite sure that I would need to.

"I am going to have Roberto set up some transmitters and spread them around the countryside. We will trigger them to go off at different times and in different locations. This will keep them on the move until we can lead them into a trap."

"What kind of trap?" Antonio asked.

"They have been playing 'cat's got your tongue' games with us, so we are going to play 'cat-and-mouse' with them," I explained. "They want to keep us in the dark, so let's keep them in the dark for a while. We will send them signals from different locations. Just as they are about to pounce in on one location, we will start transmitting from a different location. This is what they have been frustrated with so far, so I am betting they will go along with it for a spell. Right when we want to, we will lead them to a secret location and flush them out. We will be there to see it all happen. That's when we will confront them face-to-face on our terms. If they want our cooperation, they will have to let us in on what they are looking for because we know they are not looking for *narco traficantes*."

Antonio could hardly contain his enthusiasm, "That's great, *Jefe*. Where are we going to lead them to when they fall into our trap?"

"Come on with me down the hall to the engineering shop, and I'll explain as we go."

We walked down to meet Roberto, and I explained everything to both of them. I told them where to put the transmitters and how I wanted to trigger each one. They said it would only take about two days to get everything in place because Roberto had enough spare parts to build whatever I needed. Antonio and Carlos would take them each out to the locations as fast as Roberto could make them. Each one understood the time pressure that I had put them under, but they didn't fully understand why I was doing it. They thought they knew, but I didn't tell them the full story. *Padre Jesus* wasn't the only one in Choluteca using this communication tactic. I was telling them the truth, just not the complete truth … yet.

As I left them to their assignments, I wandered back through the station to check on everyone else. I started to wonder myself what this world was coming to. Could this really be the end? Were the Mayans right? Was the end date really December 21, 2012? With only a few days left, I hoped that maybe our second visit to *Ciudad Blanca* would clear things up even more. I felt that I had put in place all that I could for now, but things could change at any second. God knows the rest of the world seems to be changing every second. Why not us, too?

"*Señor* Clayton, call the operator," came the page from Carla.

I was just walking by my office, so I made a detour from my rounds and grabbed the phone.

"*Señor* Clayton, line one is *Señor* Hoggan and line two is Amaya."

"*Gracias, Carla,*" I replied as I hit line one.

"Scott, what's up?"

Scott was calling from the site at *Xhutlan* on his cell phone. "Thomas, we have to meet. We've got a lot to do in the next few days, and I'm not sure if we even know what we should be doing."

I made it short and to the point, not because Amaya was on the other line but because I felt that I could kill two birds with one stone. "Let's meet at the *Rincon* for dinner. We can go over everything." And, I thought to myself, 'I could see Amaya too'.

He agreed and I picked up line two, "Hi, *Mi Amor*. I was just on the phone with Scott. Is everything all right?"

"*Tomás*, yes, I guess . . . I"

"What's wrong, Amaya? I can tell something is not right."

"*Tomás*, it is just that with all the confusion going on, I'm starting to get scared. I want to be with you. Can you stay with me tonight, *Tomás*?"

"Amaya, you know I will. Everything will be all right I promise you. There is no need to be afraid."

"I can't help it. I don't want to wait until the holidays for us to move in. I don't want to be without you another night."

"I'm meeting Scott for dinner tonight to discuss a few things that we are working on, and I would like you to join us. I'll be there right after work around five or so. I told Scott to meet me there about six. We can have a nice long talk, the whole night long if you wish."

"Oh, *Tomás*, I knew you would understand. I feel much better now, but I'm still scared. Get here sooner if you can, *Mi Amor*."

"I will, Amaya. I will. See you soon. Love you."

She sensed the tension, along with the rest of the city. I didn't blame her. I still was not totally convinced but decided to follow *Mytar*'s instructions to listen to that inner voice and follow my feelings. It seemed that the more I let go, the more I felt. I got more in return than I gave up. I learned to trust more. That had always been hard for me.

I noticed the rain was starting outside. I had not really paid attention to the local weather reports lately, since I was more focused on the weather-related problems from other parts of the world. I finished my rounds and walked down to the newsroom to check out the weather forecasts, because it was really starting to rain heavily.

Carlos was on the air, covering for Antonio because he was still down in the shop with Roberto. Walking over to the wire service, I noticed it was time for the mid-day English newscast. Antonio popped back into the studio with Carlos just in time to deliver his report. I pushed up the volume on the newsroom console to hear what Antonio had to say.

Carlos punched up the intro, "You are listening to *Radio Onda* in Choluteca. Here's the latest news and weather with Antonio Gonzalez."

"Military helicopters continued through the night, searching for a group of suspects reported to be involved in a major drug-trafficking ring. Here is a report from," Antonio carried on as I turned my attention to another breaking story coming across the wire service. An aftershock had caused further destruction in Okinawa measuring 8.7 magnitude. It triggered two major volcanoes, Pinatubo and Mayon, in the Luzon Province of the Philippines. Reports from the area appeared to be sketchy. The only report about Okinawa was from a commercial airliner approaching the island relaying information to another air traffic controller on Midway Island. They were reporting that the international airport was closed, with no communications. Fires and dust clouds could be seen from the air and all flights into Okinawa were being diverted to Taipei, Shanghai and Nagasaki. I looked up at Carlos and motioned to him to come into the newsroom. I wanted him to get this breaking news back into Antonio before he ended his newscast.

" . . . Pacific storms are rolling in today with rain expected through tomorrow afternoon, accompanied by possible thunder and lighting later during the night. It should be a very strong but fast-moving storm. The winds will gust 30 to 40 miles per hour out of the west with rain predictions for Choluteca of 4 to 5 inches. The strongest part of the storm should hit around midnight, tapering off in the early afternoon tomorrow."

Carlos dropped the copy in front of Antonio and punched up the bulletin sounder to set Antonio up for this special report.

As I walked back to my office, I was glad to hear about the storm because the choppers would not be able to fly in this weather. That alone would buy us some time. If we had to stall more, it would all be up to us.

I decided to leave the station a little early. The storm was whipping up quite a show already. As I drove toward *El Rincon*, I called Scott on his cell phone. He had shut down everything at the site and was just about to leave for town. The storm was making Scott and me move up our time schedules. It's funny. We wanted the storm to slow down the time schedule for the military, but it was speeding up ours.

I called Tida to let her know that I would be spending the night in town with Amaya and not to worry. Tida is the only one who knew we had married. She started to go on about how she didn't understand how we could get married and continue to live apart. She scolded me and told me to bring Amaya back with me to Ranchitos and live together like man and wife. That's what I loved about Tida. She pulled no punches, called it like it should be and she was right; what could I say?

I reached *El Rincon*, parked and quickly jumped a couple of rain puddles to get up onto the covered porch area. Shaking off the rain, I nodded to Orlando, who was sitting on the bench outside the entrance feeling a little down.

"What's with the long face Orlando, *porqué es triste*?"

"When it rains, Orlando—he can't wash cars. When Orlando doesn't wash cars, he doesn't make money," he sadly replied.

"Orlando, I have a job for you. Here are my keys to my truck. You always do a good job of cleaning the outside of it. Would you clean the inside for me as well as you do the outside?

"*Sí, señor Tomás*, I can do that," Orlando said, jumping to his feet.

Handing him twenty dollars, I said, "Go down to the *Supermercado* and tell *Don Franco* what kind of job you will be doing and to provide you with all the things you will need. *Don Franco* will know and he will help you get exactly what you need to do the job."

"*Gracias, señor Tomás*. I will do a good job for you. You will see." He took the twenty and ran off down the street in the rain to the *Supermercado*.

Don Pepe was at his post as usual to greet the dinner and happy-hour crowd. I could hear the trio playing from the bar area as I walked into the *Rincon*.

"How is your *señora*?" I inquired as to *Don Pepe's* lovely wife.

"Muy bien, gracias. And how is yours?" *Don Pepe* shot back as I walked past him.

I took one more step and realized what he had just said. He had just asked how my "*señora*" or Amaya the "*wife*" was. Turning my head around to see his smiling face, I knew Amaya had confided in him. He held out his arms as I turned around to accept his warm *abrazo*.

"*Bienvenida a la familia, Don Tomás.*"

"Thank you, *Don Pepe*. I am a blessed man."

"She is so happy. I knew before she told me. I have watched her grow up since she was just a baby. She can't hide anything from her *Don Pepe*. Now she has her own man to watch over her. She, too, is lucky to have a man like you, *Don Tomás*."

"Thank you. You are very kind, *Don Pepe*."

I looked him in the eye and saw a bit of moisture. It gave his eyes a gentle little sparkle. It was a little bit of liquid soul leaking out.

Seemed like everyone in Choluteca had the same idea to knock off early and stop into the *Rincon* before heading home to ride out the storm. Amaya was at the far end of the bar talking with Lorenzo, Col. Royale and *El Alcalde*. She looked up just as I approached the group and gave me a smug smile. Enrique had his arm around Amaya's waist and they were all laughing at something.

"Enrique, if you weren't the mayor, I would have to tell you to get out of Dodge by sundown tonight for trying to steal my gal."

"You got it all backwards, partner," *El Alcalde* shot back with his best Honduran John Wayne accent, "She's my girl now!"

"That's right, Mister!" jumped in Amaya, as she hugged the mayor, slid past me in a sassy manner and headed toward the kitchen.

"Hey, this is a tough crowd," I said.

Everyone laughed. Then for a moment there was a very awkward silence. The moment flipped to a serious tone. It was unusual for this group to be this quiet. The storm was one reason to drop into *El Rincon, but* this wasn't the normal Friday night wrap-up-the-week group. This was Thursday. They were worried like everyone else about what was happening around the world and especially what was going on around here. They were edgy like the rest of us. They had all knocked off early because of the storm, but that was just the excuse that all of us seemed to be using. They were grouping or gathering together for comfort and reassurance. They say there is strength in numbers. A loud crack of thunder broke the silence.

"Looks like Antonio's report was right, *Tomás*. We're in for a long, wet night," said Lorenzo, ordering another drink and asking if I would like something.

Colonel Royale looked at me, dropping his head a little in humility and made an apology to me. "*Tomás*, I had just been telling the group that I have some major concerns for the safety of all of us here in Choluteca. The world is falling apart everywhere else. Here in Choluteca, we have always thought we were in a safe little corner of the world. Not much has affected us here in hundreds of years—maybe thousands of years—if you don't count back to when Drake and the other pirates ran us out of town. But now, I feel a little embarrassed because I found out about some things that are going on here with the military that don't add up."

Everyone's attention was on Esteban Royale, the man and friend, not Colonel Esteban Royale the Honduran Military leader of Choluteca.

"Go on Esteban," I encouraged him.

"The base at *La Semilla* is not what I was led to believe. They have some kind of secret operation going on in one of the hangers there. I don't think it is for *narco traficantes* anymore. They have been telling everyone that the helicopters are searching for drug runners. I now know that this is not true. They tell me they are running a mapping search operation. For what, I am not sure, but they are all very uptight out there. They are getting a lot of pressure from Washington to produce some results. I am afraid that they might start trying to clear out some of the jungle areas with bombs or missiles or even lasers. They have pretty much cut our government out of the equation for now. I'm afraid that I have been made a fool of, and I apologize for not knowing more. I fear for all of us right now."

"Thank you for sharing that with us, Esteban. I think we all have concerns for what is going on here in Choluteca. If we stick together, I'm sure we can get to the bottom of what they are doing. We have a couple of days; I'm sure, with this storm, before they can start up their operation again. Everything is grounded in this weather. With time on our side, we can do whatever we have to in order to protect ourselves and our families," I told the group, hoping to calm it a little.

"What can we do? They don't even know what they are looking for," said the mayor.

"I agree," said Lorenzo. "It's the not knowing that has everyone in town worried."

"We know one thing. They are picking up some kind of signal with those devices they have put out all over the place. Who is sending them and why, none of us know. I agree it's hard to fight the unknown. What we can do is not panic. And gather more information."

"How can we get that if they won't tell us anything?" asked Colonel Royale skeptically.

"We just have to ask them in a different kind of way," I said to pique their interest.

"What might that be, *Tomás*?" inquired the mayor.

"This rain will buy us a little time. As I said, I have an idea, but I will need your help and I have to tell you . . . you cannot tell a single soul. No one," I said mysteriously, leaning in toward them in a whisper for emphasis. "Not even that we are planning something. Understand?"

There was a pause as they all looked around at each other in silent agreement.

"What's your plan, Tomas?" offered Colonel Royale in an equally hush voice.

"I will let each of you know. Probably tomorrow, okay?"

Amaya came sneaking up behind me and snuggled next to me. "When you and the boys get finished talking I've got a table ready for you and Scott."

"Thanks, *Mi Amor*. I'm going to wait for Scott, but could you ask *Eduardo* if he could make me some of his special baked stuffed shrimp with his coconut cream sauce?"

"We just got in some fresh, giant tiger prawn. I'll let *Eduardo* know your request, my King," Amaya teased. "Can I get your majesty anything else?" she finished, with a playful curtsy.

"Yes, wench. My comrades are hungry, how about a sea-food platter for us to munch on?"

"Yes. Coming right up," Amaya laughed, tossing her hair back and turning to leave.

"And make it quick—my men are starving!"

El Alcalde piped up, "You, *Tomás*, are a lucky man."

That was true. For the second time in just a few minutes, others were telling me what I already knew. Some couples just project that image of togetherness and Amaya and I certainly were sharing that with each other. And I guess with everyone else, too.

The seafood platter arrived at the exact same moment Scott walked into the bar. I bid the group farewell. "*Buen provecho.*" Scott and I walked to our table and sat down.

Scott was beaming. I could tell. He had something he needed to tell me and needed to tell me quickly.

"Thomas, I've got the most incredible news. The samples that I sent overnight to Los Angeles all came back negative. The doctor called me and said all the tests are negative! He called me on my cell phone as I was driving over here. You know what that means? Lori's cancer is all gone. No more leukemia! My little girl will be all right," Scott was tearing up. "I sent multiple samples this time and they tested them all. They say they can't explain it. They have never seen anything like it before."

"Scott, that is the most positive thing I have ever heard. I am so happy for all of you."

"Robin doesn't even know yet. Nobody does because

william clyde beadles

we can't tell anyone yet, we made a promise to protect this knowledge. The doctors don't know what caused it because I didn't tell them, either. But they are curious as to what is different with Lori. They said that I should fly her up to Los Angeles, so they could study her a little more carefully. But they are absolutely sure that the leukemia is gone. They even retested the other previous samples, and they still came back clean."

"That tells us something more," I said. "The healing power of *Mytar* is true. I believe that everything he is telling us is right. We need to go back, as he has asked us. And we need to trust him in every way. We have to turn ourselves over to him and follow what he says."

"I have been a believer all along," said Scott.

"I know," I said.

"Thomas, you are convinced now, too, I can tell," replied Scott.

"This rain is going to stop tomorrow. Let's plan to go back to see *Mytar* in the afternoon. I will meet you around noon.'

"That sounds good to me," agreed Scott.

"I've got a plan in motion to help us out with a little time stalling," I went on, explaining what I had in mind. We had our dinner and then Scott left for his home to be with his family.

Almost everyone else had finished their dinners, as the restaurant was nearly empty. Most of the people now were gathered in the bar. Just as Amaya came to sit with me, we heard another loud clap of thunder and the power went out. I looked toward the windows and saw total blackness. The power to the entire town must have gone out because not even the streetlights were shining. Only the flickering of the candles and the light from the fire pit illuminated the room. I heard some cheering from the bar. They were really getting into it; both the liquor and the storm.

"*Tomás*, I feel safe with you here."

"I love the rain and the thunder. It's very romantic especially the way your eyes dance with the flickering of the candlelight," I told her as I stood up. "Would you care to dance, wench?"

"Ay, *Capitán* Drake, it would be my pleasure," Amaya played along, standing up to embrace me. The music was still coming from the bar.

We did a few turns and I whispered in her ear. "Tell *Eduardo* to close up and let's go to bed."

I put my arm around her waist and we walked out to the patio. As we passed the kitchen, Amaya shouted out orders, "*Eduardo*, you heard the *Capitán*!"

"No, senorita, I did not," replied a puzzled *Eduardo* from the kitchen.

"He said you are in charge of the ship and we are off to our bunks!"

"*Buenas Noches!*" *Eduardo* yelled back with laughter in his voice.

The full brunt of the tropical Pacific storm was upon us now. We scooted along the covered interior patio walkway as the lightning and thunder surrounded us. We made it across the courtyard to the entrance to Amaya's and, I guess, my house now, too. Amaya's housekeeper had already lit candles, so we could find our way. We shook off the rain that managed to slightly drench us and went straight to the bedroom.

"I'm going right into a hot shower. Do you want to join me?" Amaya said, as she grabbed one of the candles off her dresser and went into the bathroom.

"I just had one!" I replied still dripping from our walk over from the restaurant.

"Yeah, but did you wash behind your ears, *mi hijo*?" Amaya charmed back.

I looked up for a moment and replied, "You got me there. Here I come."

CHAPTER 13

When I woke up, I noticed Amaya was already up and gone. She was out taking care of breakfast. It was still raining, but the thunder and lightning had gone away. I got dressed and went out to meet Amaya for breakfast.

Later, I stopped by the station to organize my guys to go out and set up the transmitters. When I finished, it was almost noon, so I headed out to meet Scott at *Xhutlan*.

When I pulled into Scott's compound, I saw Raul waiting for me. He tipped his hat and smiled. I jumped down into the mud and walked over to the porch to get out of the rain.

Raul had a hot mug of coffee in his hand and offered me one as he told me, "Scott is down in the Temple of *K'in* working. He said to bring you over when you got here."

I thanked Raul for the coffee and asked, "Have you seen any troops around here, Raul?"

"Last night, nothing but rain. The night before, they were flying helicopters over the north and west sides of Choluteca. We had one group of soldiers try to come in here three days ago, but I ran them off. I told them they did not have permission to come on this site. They put up a little protest, but they finally left. That night, I saw another of those silent jets hovering around the area, but they only stayed for a few minutes and then they slipped off."

"Thanks again for the coffee," I told Raul, as I looked out over the meadow at the Temple of *K'in*. Just at that moment, I saw the rays of *K'in* cutting through the clouds, letting *Chak* know it was time to take his rain and go home. It was only patchy clouds now with spotty rain. I put down my cup and told Raul, "Let's go."

Walking through the muddy meadow to the temple, the sun was bursting through the clouds above and the jungle steam was rising like more clouds out of the earth. These floor clouds were created from the coolness of the rain falling on the warm earth. It was the energy of *K'in*, changing rain into floor clouds, to be sent back into the sky for *Chak* to gather up and play with on another rainy day. I felt gathering anticipation with each footstep. I was about to enter the temple for the second time. I did not have the anxiety or fear of my first visit. I walked confidently toward the entrance with a new respect, a new knowledge and a new excitement of what we were about to discover.

The Temple of *K'in* was waiting for me. The storm had washed down all the dust and the temple gleamed in the sun. It seemed to take on a new look. *K'in* knew that we were friends. The temple looked inviting, less intimidating than before, the green of the tangled vines sparkled like living emerald bracelets encircling the building blocks of the temple. The droplets of rain covered the leaves like sparking tears of joy laid down by the *Chak* ,God of rain. I felt the presence of unseen ancient Mayan temple workers standing proudly around the base of this magnificent structure.

As Raul walked ahead of me to the entrance, I stopped for a moment to look around. A slight wind brushed across the meadow. The jungle surrounding it reminded me of a fortress with each tree and palm making up the living walls. The hills rising out of the jungle nearby were still partly covered in clouds. The forest noises had returned and life was coming out of every hiding place from where it had taken shelter from the storm. Blossoming plants drank from the tropical rain. Their brilliant petals and fragrant scents again filled the jungle with both color and perfume. I was alive with sensations.

I took in a long, deep, fresh breath of air and reminded myself of just how beautiful life really was. I was in such a hurry to get to where I was going that I felt I had to stop for a moment and let my soul catch up with me. I needed to remember that the journey is the reward. The end of this journey is just the beginning of your next one.

Mytar was right. I was beginning to get in touch with my inner self and with that small voice inside of me. I was listening to and feeling life. I was breathing life back into myself. It was a spiritual feeling—something that I had not experienced very often in my life. Whenever I did, it would just come and go. This was different. I sensed the presence of this inner spiritual feeling, not as part of me, but part of something or someone else that was within me. It was also beside me, in front of me, all around me. It was a comfort. It was with me. All I had to do was to recognize its presence and I could feel it. It was like a guardian angel or spirit that protected and rewarded me with a feeling of calm and comfort. It was my inner compass telling me which way to go. It was a life force of positive energy.

I turned once more and walked to Raul. We entered through the portal and climbed down into the chamber to meet Scott. Sitting atop the bolder, he was looking down at the wall mural. I climbed the carved hand and footholds to the top to join him. Raul stayed below.

Scott with his laptop opened, was deep in thought just staring at the wall. He didn't even notice that I had joined him. I sat next to him without saying a word and looked down at the wall. This was only the second time that I had seen it. It was still a wall of wonderment. This time, I tried not to look at the wall, but to open myself and let the wall absorb me. It was so quiet here. I began to feel a sound. Not hear it, but feel it. It was a slow, pulsating rhythm. Not a steady pulse. It seemed to have different frequencies and waves of rhythms. It was almost like it had its own language.

All of a sudden, I was aware that the wall was talking to me. Not with words for my ears, but communicating with me nonetheless. The wall had motion and depth. It wasn't the two dimensions that I had experienced before. I was now experiencing what we had learned from *Mytar*. The fourth dimension was present somewhat like a virtual reality experience but more real. I now understood what the wall was. It was the explanation of Mayan time from the beginning of the first cycle to the end of the fifth. It explained the progression to the next dimensions and outlined each one in my mind up through the sixth. That is when it stopped for me. I couldn't go beyond the sixth dimension. *Mytar* would still have to teach us and lead us through the instructions for the final six. I was convinced that we had to get to *Mytar* soon. We needed to know exactly why we had to protect this knowledge for a few more days and what he expected us to do.

I looked over to Scott. He was right next to me but, at the same time, light years away. He was consumed by the wall like I had been. I watched him for a few more minutes and then he turned to me.

"When did you get here?" he asked me.

"I've been here. *You* just got back!" I told him.

"What do you mean?" he asked.

"I climbed up here about an hour ago, and you were sitting exactly where you are now. You were staring at the wall, deep in thought; so, I started to look at the wall and soon I was absorbed by it too. Did it come alive for you, too?" I was anxious to get his reaction.

"It's unbelievable. It brought everything that *Mytar* has taught us so far to life. I couldn't go any further that the sixth dimension."

"Me either!"

"Thomas, we have to go to *Mytar*," said Scott as he looked back at the wall again.

"I know. We need to go right now! We have to know the rest of the story. The storm is over outside." And without another word, we scrambled down the stone boulder and climbed out of the chamber into the sunlight.

As we walked across the damp meadow, I noticed *Utmal* standing on the edge of the clearing.

He knew we were coming. News travels instantaneously in the fourth dimension. He walked with us straight to the boulder. This time we didn't even break our stride as we walked into the boulder and onto *Ciudad Blanca*.

Mytar stood waiting for us at the entrance to the market. He welcomed us and asked us to follow him. We walked without conversation through the market and out into the fields surrounding the city. We came to what looked like an ancient stone amphitheater. It wasn't large, maybe enough for 200 people. But now, it was just the four of us. *Mytar* asked us to sit down on one of the stone benches.

Mytar began. "I know that you have absorbed everything that I have taught you so far. This knowledge will be with you forever, as I told you before. This is the promise. Now I will give you a glance into the next six dimensions." With that, he waved his hand in a slow, curved motion up over his head. As he did, the outdoor amphitheater turned into an indoor planetarium. The canopy, like a darkened sky, followed the motion of his hand, covering over the arena with a roof. I could see stars, planets, comets, the full moon and the Milky Way. Not like a make-believe sky you see in a planetarium. *Mytar* had turned day into night right in front of our eyes. It was incredible.

He stood before us. "We have been guarding this earthly planet for many years from invading objects that could have caused real damage to this delicate world we live in on earth. Look at the face of the moon. It is battle-scarred. We had a close call a few years back, but we were able to send it onto Jupiter for the world to see what could have happened here on this earth if we had collided. The seventh dimension has control of negative problems in the universe that might impact our earth."

Just then I saw a giant fireball heading toward us from outer space. *Mytar* held out his hand and the object shot across the sky, missing us. "You will be able to do the same. Whether it is an object, a ray or a solar wind. The seventh dimension is the force to deal with threatening elements."

"With the eighth dimension, you will be able to travel anywhere in your solar system." At that moment, we were standing on the moon, next to the flag that was planted there many years before by visiting American astronauts. "Man has been attempting for centuries to do what we just did in the twinkling of an eye. Some of those early astronauts got a peek at the forth dimension. They were allowed a taste of what was in store for all mankind."

I looked back and saw earth.

Mytar said, "Turn around."

As we did, I noticed the terrain now was sandy red and I saw part of a pyramid protruding from the ground. I turned back to look at *Mytar* and said, "Are we on Mars?" I felt like a kid on Christmas with a new magical computer travel game.

"Scott, I know you are wondering how this pyramid got here. Let's just say for now that those who once lived here have moved on," said *Mytar*, reading Scott's thoughts.

I looked to the heavens again to see Earth as a small bluish dot and the sun much smaller than on Earth. I was humbled at my own worth in comparison to the rest of the universe.

"*Tomás*, just as you are a speck in this solar system," *Mytar* interjected reading my mind, "the solar system is just a speck in the universe."

We were on the move again. I was watching our sun, all the planets and the asteroids turning in space, getting smaller and smaller. We had left our solar system, and now I was seeing others like, yet not like ours.

Mytar explained that in the ninth dimension, we would be free to explore other worlds. We would be able to override the eighth dimension that only allowed us to move around in our own solar system. The ninth dimension gave us the power to escape our own solar boundaries. Our sun would no longer control our gravitational pull. For a moment, I felt like the early ocean explorers who felt that they might sail off the edge of the earth and into space. We were literally sailing off the edge of our solar system and into the universe. Infinity surrounded us.

Mytar looked over to Scott and said, "The possibilities are endless. The opportunities cannot be counted. Someday, you will be given the architectural keys to the universe for the tenth dimension. With those tools, you will be able to physically create your own solar system. Instead of studying the ruins of the past, you will be the architect of the future. And it will be your own special future; exactly the way you want to design it."

"What about life itself?" Scott asked.

"The eleventh dimension," *Mytar* responded. "With this dimension, you and your spouse will equally share in the creation, design and production of life for your new world. What you both create you will be responsible for and will suffer and rejoice in their tragedies and triumphs."

"And the twelfth dimension?" I anxiously asked knowing it was the final one for us to know.

"Before I answer the twelfth, I want you to return to the first three with me again. Turn around," *Mytar* commanded.

As Scott and I turned around, we were startled to find that we were standing in front of the great asteroid mirror surface in the chamber of the temple of *K'in*. We were back on Earth. Three dimensions. The riddle of the asteroid had been answered. It was a portal into the universe. It only reflected life. Life was the only thing that was really transportable. Everything else could be created.

"The twelfth dimension is the final dimension. It is not an end. It is the true beginning. It is the absolute knowledge of all things past, present and future. It is not perfect. But it is the secret to progression. The twelfth dimension is what some have called the meaning of life. It is the intelligence, power and knowledge of all things. It may seem flawless, but the truth is that there is no such thing as perfection. Just progression. You will encounter situations and opposition, just like on Earth. Many pious souls have placed all their energies toward the quest for perfection. If all things were perfect, we would have no progression. The goal is not the prize. The journey is the reward. And because the journey is never ending, so are the rewards. It is really quite simple when you think about it."

"The Maya are from another time. We have been sent here to this earth to teach the dimensions. We are the time-keepers assigned to Earth in her last days. This world has progressed as far as it can. The world is falling apart and the people have lost sight of what they were sent here for. It is time for the earth and everyone on it to enter into a new dimension. The time for this, as you know, is tomorrow, with the winter solstice. This will be the end of the final cycle and the end of your world, as you know it. Tomorrow will be the transition and the beginning of a new phase in the progression of mankind.   The architect of this solar system will send his teachers to open a period of cleansing, learning and trust, in preparation of the beginning of the next period of progression. Those who surrender—I don't mean surrender in a negative way, but rather in a positive way—by turning themselves over to their God, will find the way to eternal enrichment. There is only one God of this universe. He goes by many names. We, the Maya, call him *K'in*. He has sent many teachers through the ages to help with the progression of this life. They will arrive tomorrow. It is your job to focus the attention to the meadows of *Xhutlan*. You must do it, so the world will be focused on this location. Hold off the armies, but allow the people to come. You will be safe there, as will your families."

"*Utmal* and I need to return. Now you have the whole story, except for one thing, *Tomás*. I have told you about the twelve dimensions and the promise. Now the final piece of knowledge: the warning. I will give that to you both tomorrow."

Mytar and *Utmal* turned and entered the portal and were gone. All we saw were our reflections and the endless universe beyond our reflections.

william clyde beadles

CHAPTER 14

With all of the things going on in the world, you would think that I should be scared to death, but I wasn't. I was extraordinarily calm and confident. By now, I had a very good idea about what was about to come. I, like Scott, had reached the point where we knew that we were powerless. I had surrendered myself to God, and I was willing to do anything that was asked of me.

I had struggled all my life with the thought that I could make a difference, and in some little ways, I'd like to think that I did. But the power trips that others had taken in their lives were not for me. That is the main reason I dropped out from the big leagues and came to Honduras. The world had become too chaotic, too commercial, too '*me, me, me*'. People had become so self-centered they would do nothing unless there was something in it for them. Yes, they played around like they were interested with different causes. But even the causes became corrupt. Power struggles and money ruled. People all over the world were going through the motions, but not really devoting themselves to their causes. Sure, there were a few, but what I am talking about is the vast majority of people everywhere. They had lost sight of values and family. Of compassion and trust. Love was just a marketing tool used to entice, persuade and sell.

The world was falling apart because of a loss in direction and values. Terrorism, war, corruption, greed and envy. Drugs, alcohol and gang mentality had become the addictions of the day. People attacked themselves with their own addictions and destroyed the lives of those around them. Yes, there were the gangs in the streets, but also gangs of lawyers, gangs of clergy, gangs of politicians, gangs of physicians, gangs of terrorists—all creating their own brand of chaos. Even families were dividing themselves into different factions. The whole concept of families had basically collapsed. Right from wrong seemed to blend together. It was a world confused, without direction, lacking in morals, integrity and respect. It was now a world in decay where almost anything could be rationalized. The entire world seemed to be in denial. What the world needed was a wake-up call, a return to sanity. The world needed to be checked into a detox center.

All of these reasons were why I left, finding in Honduras a lifestyle more like what I thought it should be. What life used to be. But I realized that even in Honduras there was no escape. Instead I had learned to follow my inner self and find peace from within even though I was surrounded by chaos.

Scott and I, along with my men, worked through the night to set and check all the hidden transmitters. We separated just before sunrise to go and get our families and to meet at the meadows of *Xhutlan*.

During the night, the power emissions that *Mytar* had told us about began to direct all the magnetic north compasses in the world to all point to our general direction. It was as if the magnetic north was now right here in Honduras. Worldwide communications were on again-off again. No signal or broadcast maintained its integrity. All commercial aircraft had been temporally grounded because of all this confusion. The world was quickly beginning to focus its attention on Honduras. Intense pressure was being placed on the troops here to discover at any cost what was occurring in this region.

Mytar said the transmissions would increase in intensity until the sun was directly overhead in the sky. Then it would stop. After a brief silence, "It" would begin. Just what "It" was, he did not say. He didn't need to. Scott and I already knew.

During the night, the military had closed down all the borders sealing off the main roads into Honduras from El Salvador and Nicaragua. The government had moved in troops to cover the main arteries in and out of Choluteca. They had basically surrounded the area. No one was able to leave or get in unless they tried to parachute in or climb up out of the ground. We were sealed off from the world. The military was convinced that whatever was going on all around the world was because of what was happening here. They still didn't know what, but they were confident the answer laid in finding out who was sending the transmissions and why.

The joint forces of U.S. Marines and the Honduran military were checking all movement on the roads, looking for anything or anyone that might give them a clue as to what was happening in the area.

I told Carlos to go back to the station and give Roberto any assistance that he might need in starting the activation of the transmitters we had hidden. I told Antonio to bring our remote broadcast truck out to the site at *Xhutlan* and wait for me there.

I drove to *Los Ranchitos* to pick up Amaya and Bark. I left her there with Tida while I was out with the guys during the night. I knew she would feel safe there, even though I wasn't with her. I didn't take the main streets through town because the troops were everywhere and checking everything. I took a bumpy dirt road that skirted the Rio Choluteca. All I saw were some of the women washing clothes along the riverbank. Once I passed the cemetery, I was able to join the main road west of town, evading the roadblocks.

As I pulled up to our house, I saw Bark run out to greet me. Amaya was standing in the archway of the front patio. Her long dark, wet, hair flowing down her terrycloth robe, she was fresh from her morning shower. She was just sipping her morning coffee.

"Honey, get dressed fast. We have to go!" I called out to her.

"What's the matter?" she said with concern.

"I'll explain on the way. Just get dressed and get in the truck! I'll tell Tida," I said as I walked quickly past her and back to the kitchen.

We were back on the road in a matter of minutes.

"Okay, what's this all about?" Amaya said with a nervous voice.

"It's all okay, honey. We just . . ." I hit a washed out pothole and the truck swerved slightly. "We just found something very interesting out at the site where Scott has been working, and we wanted to share it with everyone." I still couldn't even tell my wife. Scott and I had to defend the secret right to the end.

"Well, slow down then. Why are you so excited?'

Sheepishly, I replied, "Well, it is very exciting. I need to get there as soon as possible. Scott and Antonio are waiting for me. And the military is everywhere, conducting some kind of search for those drug traffickers. They've got road blocks everywhere."

I took the cutoff to the cemetery again to avoid the road-blocks into town. As I dropped down to the old river road, we ran right into a foot patrol. I slowed down and looked out to see that big tall Montana cowboy leading the group.

"Edmunds, right?" I spoke first.

"Yes, sir. You are the radio owner," he remembered me.

"What's going on today?"

"We are on full alert or something. They think something is about to happen and we are patrolling, looking for anything or anyone suspicious. Suspicious of what I'm not sure. We are in radio contact with the base. From what I have been hearing, they are getting close to finding what we are supposed to be looking for. Radio is breaking up a lot today for some reason. They mainly want us to patrol the river's edge."

"We are on our way to see my friend, Scott. Hope you find what you are looking for," I said as I started to pull off.

Edmunds grinned and rolled his eyes back. I heard him say, "Thanks, sir" as we left them in my rear view mirror.

We were stopped once more, as we pulled back up to town to catch the Pan American Highway north across the bridge. From there on, it was smooth sailing. The cutoff to the meadows of *Xhutlan* was not blocked by the military. We still had time. I had to get the transmitters operating right away.

As we pulled up in front of Scott's office at the site, I told Amaya, "I have to talk to Antonio and Scott. Take Bark with you and stay here with Robin and the kids."

Robin and Raul were cooking up breakfast for everyone. Amaya and Bark walked over onto the porch to join them. I walked over to the transmitter station truck where Antonio and Scott were talking. Just then, overhead two helicopters shot by in formation at a high rate of speed. They crossed over us heading northeast toward the hills.

"We're all ready, *Jefe*. Roberto is standing by at the station. He says they are having a lot of interference with our radio station's signal today. He's not sure what it is, says he's never seen anything like it before. He's been getting phone calls from media services all over the world wanting to know what is going on down here. But he is ready for us," said Antonio.

"Don't worry about the station for right now. Let's get the field transmitters working," I told him.

"Can I help with anything?" asked Scott.

"Yeah, I have a strange feeling about the chamber. Go down there and see if everything is the same. I am feeling a strong pull coming from there."

Scott looked me in the eyes and smiled. "I know. I'm feeling it, too."

Scott turned and walked toward the temple of *K'in*. I explained to Antonio how I wanted the sequence to go on the transmitters. "Send out a random series of tones. Start with the first transmitter for three minutes. Then, in random order after a five-minute break, set off the next transmitter, followed by another break and then another transmitter. After you have finished all 12 locations fire all of them randomly and continuously for 10 to 20 seconds each. I want to keep them focused on hunting down the signals. Remember—like a 'cat and mouse' game. Keep them on the run. On the hour, go totally silent for five minutes and then start the sequence all over again."

Antonio, looking a little confused, jumped in, "I'm not sure I got all of that."

"Don't worry about making a mistake, Antonio. There is no reasoning to the sequence. The more confusing it is; the more confusing it will be to the military."

"Okay, I think I've got, it, *Jefe*."

In a reassuring voice, I told Antonio, "Just follow your gut. Have some fun with it. Remember, *you* are controlling *them*. If you have any problems, remember that Roberto is standing by at the station, okay?"

Scott ran out from the entrance to the temple and yelled. "Thomas! Thomas, come over here."

"I know you can do it, Antonio, I've gotta go."

I ran over to meet Scott at the entrance to the temple.

"They are here!" Scott blurted out.

"They who?"

"*Mytar, Utmal* and the rest!"

"The rest?"

"You know . . . the others . . . never mind—just come in with me," Scott told me, motioning to hurry.

I stumbled along behind Scott, through the entrance tunnel to the opening of the chamber. At first I was so amazed at the transition of the chamber I hardly noticed who was present. The wall mural was alive with color, light and motion. It had depth and three dimensions. The stone clock was operating in all of its splendorous glory. *Mytar* was atop the boulder on the observation platform, directing the actions of the others. *Utmal* was positioned at the bottom of the steps waiting for us. All of the others were running the wall mural as if it were a giant control board. *Mytar* motioned to us to join him atop the platform.

There was tremendous excitement and energy in the air. It was hard to hold back or contain my own excitement and anticipation. Scott and I reached the top of the boulder and greeted *Mytar*.

He acknowledged that we were there, but he was consumed in directing his people. None of us spoke a word for a couple of minutes. Both Scott and I were just soaking in all of the energy and motion going on around us. It seemed as if *Mytar* was tuning in everything as if the entire room was a giant transmitter. I knew there were multi-dimensions at work here. I could feel it. The little we had experienced, up until now at least, made me aware of the possibilities. For now, I felt comfortable just knowing I was not totally lost. Multi-dimensional living was going to take a little getting used to.

Mytar paused and looked over to Scott and me. "Everything is in place. This is the day we have been waiting for. Go now and join your families. It is about to begin. I will join you in the meadows."

I walked out of the temple. The sunlight hit me hard. I stopped for a moment to let my eyes adjust. My ears perked up just like Bark's would. I heard jets screaming toward our direction, closing in at a high rate of speed. They were coming in from over Choluteca. I looked up to see a blur streak past me, flying just above the trees. I looked over to the left and saw two helicopters flying toward the same direction the jets were headed. The 'cat and mouse' games had begun. I walked over to my truck to see how Antonio was doing.

"You've been missing the show, *Jefe*. The transmitters are working well. They are flying all over the damn place," Antonio excitedly reported. "They're looking everywhere but here!"

"That's exactly what we wanted," I told him.

I looked over to see Scott's kids playing with Bark. Stephen was running barefoot with Bark. He had taken off his socks and put a rock in the toe of one of them. He tied a knot in it so the rock wouldn't fly out. He was slinging it out into the meadows for Bark to retrieve. It was great to see little Lori chasing right behind her little brother, laughing and yelling beneath the sun. She was experiencing no pain. Once again, she was a young vibrant child of God. I looked down at my watch and saw it was 11:45 a.m. *Mytar* said it would begin at noon. I have to admit I was ready for it.

Just then, off toward the mountains, I heard two explosions. One followed by another. I wasn't sure what it was, but it was easy to guess. One of those pilots finally saw something and fired on it. I ran back over to Antonio.

"What's going on?" I asked.

"They just took out one of the transmitters," Antonio quickly replied. "They probably think they stopped it."

"That's great. Give it about five minutes then start up the next closest transmitter and lead them further away. If they blow that one away, fire off another one!" I told him. "Just keep them on the run!"

As I walked back to Scott's office to meet Amaya and the rest, I noticed the meadow was filling will people, thousands of people from the city and the countryside. *Mytar* said they would come. They surrounded the meadow and the temple of *K'in*. They all looked like they were in a peaceful trance. As I walked toward the porch, Amaya ran out to meet me.

"Is everything okay?" she asked.

"Everything is just fine," I said to her as I took her in my arms and gave her a soft hug. "Everything is just fine."

"Why are all of these people here?"

"They are here to join us. Something very special is about to be revealed."

"Thomas, will it be good?"

"Yes, Amaya, it will be good."

No sooner had I said these reassuring words when out of the east screamed two jets. They passed directly over us then climbed up into the clouds. Once in the clouds, they went into silent mode. The deafening roar stopped dead. I looked off to the clouds to the west and I saw them and two others. Now they were four. Hovering just below the clouds, they waited. They were just there staring at us. For one split second, I started to feel a tightness in my stomach. They had locked in on our transmissions from our field truck transmitter. Before I could let that thought grow, they launched four missiles directly at us. Out of the corner of my eye, I saw *Mytar* emerge from the temple. He stretched out his hand and all the incoming missiles exploded at once, halfway between the jets and us. At the same time the missiles exploded everything went black. I immediately thought . . . wait, is this "It"? There was no sound. There was no sight. It was pitch black. I was still here. Amaya was still in my arms. Nothing else seemed to exist. I wasn't scared, just momentarily confused. *Mytar* knew what was going on and I was sure this was just the beginning of what he described.

"It" was indeed beginning.

I held Amaya tightly in my arms. She was shivering in fright. I tried to reassure her the best I could. Talking slowly and calmly, I told her, "Everything is okay. Everything is okay. I know what is happening and it is good. Relax, breathe a deep breath. That's good. Keep going. Don't worry. Look me in the face."

In the darkness, even though I couldn't see her, I could feel her starting to relax. Still holding on to me for dear life, her shivering stopped. I could tell she was trying to look me in the face, even though she couldn't see me. I could feel her breath on my face in the darkness, and I knew we were looking each other in the eyes even though neither of us could see anything. I didn't need to see her face. I could see her with my eyes closed if I wanted to. I could see her spiritually even though I couldn't see her physically. I could actually see her. I didn't need light. *Mytar* told me I would be able to see without looking . . . without my eyes. Eyes were only three-dimensional. The gifts *Mytar* gave me were starting to kick in. They were multi-dimensional.

"Thomas, are you really there?" Amaya said almost believing I wasn't.

"Yes, *Mi Amor*. I am here," I reassured her. Just hearing my voice was calming—I could tell. I held her tightly against my chest. Our arms were so tightly entwined, I felt as if we were one. Our souls were comforting each other in the fourth dimension.

"There is nothing to fear," I whispered in her ear. "We are about to witness the greatest awakening ever. Our lives are not over; it's just a new beginning into a new age. A new age of love, understanding, progress—of marvelous things to come. We are at the beginning of a new journey."

Everything was very quiet. In the darkness, everything was gone or at least appeared to be gone. It was as if Amaya and I were the only things left. We were all that existed. We were one. Even though we were separate souls, we were joined together in purpose. We were soul mates, as they used to say. Only now I knew what that phrase meant.

"Look up!" I suddenly saw the sky was filled with stars. The darkness had been pierced. Around me, I could see Scott with his family, *Padre Jesus*, the mayor, the ranchers, even some of the soldiers. They were all there. They all appeared calm and were all standing together, gazing off into the heavens. The light from the stars and the Milky Way gave off just enough light to leave everything in silhouettes. The stars were actually very bright but soft, pale shades of blue-white. The heavens around them were dark, deep black.

I always thought the stars were white, but now they were actually an incredible, intense, pure blue white.

Over the horizon, I could see a brightness growing. I could see the foothills drenched in shadows with *Las Montañas de Soledad* off to the northeast. The full moon popped up over them rising quickly, as if it were a balloon. Within a few seconds, it was in full splendor near Polaris, the North Star. Hanging in the sky, its motion stopped, the moon was suspended as if it were a wall hanging pegged to the sky for all to admire.

Directly overhead, a small intense light began to grow from a pinpoint to a dimension twice the size of the moon. It was the sun. It was *K'in*. As it grew, it was as if we were experiencing the dawn of a new day as the night sky turned into daylight within seconds. Not only did the sun grow in size, but also in brightness. The radiant light went from its normal yellow to a pure white. Its brightness was just as blinding as the darkness had been. We had to cover our eyes with our hands. The brightness could not be shut out. The light was piercing. The light was so powerful it felt that we were about to be consumed by fire or that we might just burst into flames. But there was no heat. No sense of fear. It was warm and calming. We were being bathed in *K'in's* light. The intensity of the light began to subside and as it did, we heard a voice. I could not tell where it came from, only that it was from above. At the time we didn't know it, but every living person on earth was experiencing this same phenomenon. Everyone heard Him speak and they all heard Him speak in their own language. Everyone was experiencing the same thing at the same time.

"I am here. I have always been here. I am with you. I am you. You may have, at times, felt you were without me. It was you who left. Even though you have said that I was gone, I was still with you. Your lives are about to change in a magnificent and wonderful way. Your strength and power are derived by your love. You are now ready to learn the ways of the next cycle of progression. Long ago I sent my messengers to help you, guide you and encourage you through your journey on this earth. They are returning here now. They are my teachers. I also have others that have been waiting to help you through this next transition. Hear them all. Follow them. Learn what they have to give you. They bring you gifts beyond which you have not even begun to dream of. The light is the way. It is the source. It is the cleansing element that bonds life together. Receive them and you will receive the light and the answers to everything. They are here. Receive them."

With that, out of the brightness of the sun descended three images. They each looked directly at me as if they were only looking at me. Amaya, Scott and everyone else felt the same thing. They were looking at all of us at the same time but, as if they were just looking at us one-on-one. As the three came into sight and set down in the meadows of *Xhutlan*, I could finally make out just whom the three teachers were. One was Buddha. One was Jesus Christ. One was Mohammed.

Three of the greatest teachers the world had ever known. Just as they touched the earth, the jungle behind them began to transform. We watched while it changed in front of us consuming us into the fourth dimension. *Ciudad Blanca* appeared. The entire Mayan population that had been saved throughout the ages to come forward on this day was walking toward us. They would be our guides and The Three would be our teachers.

They had been with us all along over the past few thousand years, but in another dimension preparing to lead us into the future. They would teach all of us, as Scott and I had been taught, about what marvelous things were waiting for us. This was my answer to where the intellectual power of the ancient kings of the rainforest had gone. They were chosen to be the guides of this world into the next.

All of the people who had gathered in the meadow began to walk toward The Three. Everyone was together. Everyone was equal. There was no one-and-only answer to man's search for God. We had all tried to find Him in our own way. He loved us all. Every man, woman and child were important to Him. *We* had tried to complicate religion and life. Yet, all along, it was all around us. It was simple. It was pure. It was Him. Christ, Buddha and Mohammed all taught the same basic truth. They each had their own approach. But their ultimate goal was the same—to help us find our way through the journey of life, so we could one day find our way back to God.

As I held Amaya in my embrace, I looked around and saw the love, the caring and the peacefulness that was being demonstrated throughout this crowd of humanity. The so called end of the world was not an angry God pouring out his wrath upon mankind. It was not the apocalypse or Armageddon so much portrayed in the minds of modern day evangelists.

It was simply an end of one era or time and the beginning of another. It was not chaos. It was a time to end the chaos. It was time for harmony. It was a time to stop the madness and be cleansed with the truth. The more complicated we made life the further away from it we ran. The world had lost its direction and was floundering on self destruction. There was no reason to continue on in the direction the world was heading. It was a time for a new beginning. A time to learn another way.

Our journey through this life had come to an end. We were about to embark on a new journey. The Mayan count-down was over.

I looked one more time toward the direction of *Mytar*. He was standing at the entrance to the temple of *K'in*. He stood tall and erect. He beamed with joy. His mission had been successful. He had arrived at his new beginning, too.

Mytar was true to his last word. Progression was endless. Timeless. The spirit or soul was intelligent energy. It was not perfect, either. We were still our own worst enemies, even with all that knowledge. Even with the knowledge of all things, we were still capable of doing something more, of doing something that was still hard for me to accept, even though I knew it was true.

This was the warning: *Along with total knowledge and power also comes the ability to destroy it all.*

william clyde beadles

EPILOGUE

You are probably wondering where I am today, and why I am telling you this story. I am somewhere where you have not arrived yet.

It's true that all of this happened. It just hasn't happened to you yet.

Just keep in mind; December 21, 2012 is just around the corner for you. I've already been there.

Remember that I always wanted to find that big story, well, it found me. Now that I have shared it with you, enjoy it and share it with others. Prepare your lives now, and you will enjoy the experience even more. Scott and I were lucky. We knew ahead of time. This is a gift I give to you.

My now is my now. Your now is your now. Take care of your's now, and the rest will take care of itself.

Life really isn't that difficult to figure out. Just look beyond what you see. Listen beyond what you can hear. Feel beyond what you can feel. Go ahead. Stretch your imagination. Now, just look a little beyond that. There it is . . . .

—*Thomas Clayton*

william clyde beadles

Photo by Scott Beadles

ABOUT THE AUTHOR

William Clyde Beadles is an accomplished, award winning international writer and journalist. His first Mayan experience was at age 19, wandering around in fascination of the Mayan ruins at Copan in Honduras. William has worked, lived and traveled throughout Latin America. He is an MBA graduate from the Thunderbird School of Global Management with a BA in Journalism from the University of Hawaii. Currently living in the Rocky Mountains of Utah, he enjoys trout fishing, exploring ghost towns, gourmet cooking and travel.

2012mayancountdown@gmail.com